She started reading again with determination. History was her most important subject. While math was the most difficult, the teacher in that class didn't matter to her. Miss O'Brien mattered. It mattered that she appeared well-versed, articulate, even brilliant in Miss O'Brien's class. She wanted those sea-green eyes to crinkle into hers in laughter, admiration. She wanted to hear her say . . .

Suddenly all of her senses were tuned to the person who had just entered. Ruby's eyes did not leave the book. Rather, they became fixed on the jumbled print. She was totally aware of the long, well-shaped legs in their knee-length socks, moving up the aisle with that arrogant grace that every teen-aged boy in Harlem tried to emulate. The tweed skirt brushed Ruby in passing, and she inhaled to breathe the subtle fragrance in which the girl walked.

ROSA GUY has written many distinguished books for young adults, including *The Disappearance*, *New Guys Around the Block*, and *Edith Jackson*, all available in Laurel-Leaf editions. A founder of the Harlem Writer's Guild, Rosa Guy lives in New York City.

ALSO AVAILABLE IN LAUREL-LEAF BOOKS:

THE DISAPPEARANCE, *Rosa Guy*
NEW GUYS AROUND THE BLOCK, *Rosa Guy*
EDITH JACKSON, *Rosa Guy*
VISION QUEST, *Terry Davis*
HOOPS, *Walter Dean Myers*
THE OUTSIDE SHOT, *Walter Dean Myers*
ACE HITS THE BIG TIME, *Barbara Beasley Murphy*
    and *Judie Wolkoff*
FLY LIKE AN EAGLE, *Barbara Beasley Murphy*
THE DEAR ONE, *Jacqueline Woodson*
A SUMMER LIFE, *Gary Soto*

Published by
Bantam Doubleday Dell Books for Young Readers
a division of
Bantam Doubleday Dell Publishing Group, Inc.
1540 Broadway
New York, New York 10036

RUBY

Rosa Guy

Published by
Bantam Doubleday Dell Books for Young Readers
a division of
Bantam Doubleday Dell Publishing Group, Inc.
1540 Broadway
New York, New York 10036

ISBN: 0-440-21130-1

RL: 4.7

Reprinted by arrangement with the author

Printed in the United States of America

January 1992

10 9 8 7 6 5 4 3
OPM

To my sister
Ameze

PART ONE

PART ONE

1

Loneliness, like a vapor, wafted from her bowels up through her stomach, encompassed her heart where, gaining substance, it slithered along her throat, collecting, thickening, making the cords bulge out on her neck, forcing her to swallow, hold on to the thickness, prevent its erupting into screams, hysteria, torrents of tears. She really had nothing to cry about. Looking through the window, Ruby's brown, brown eyes soulfully studied the intricate designs on the brownstones across the street—tiny, beautiful designs, carved into stone, details that told the story of once-upon-a-time.

Her eyes turned once again to look at the moving van, into which men were packing furniture, the van that would take Marian and her family away from their lives forever. A life style of New York, this constant moving: from one house or apartment to another, from one street to another, one borough to another, and sometimes out of the city forever. This surely must be even truer here in Harlem. So many had moved from the neighborhood, from this street, which she had found so lovely, so impressive when she had first come there from the Island—was it only two years ago?

The moving of the Robbinses was no great loss, and so there was no need for tears. Her and her sister's relationship with Marian had been quickly established and as quickly spent. Friendships were like that in this country —fluid as water, fragile as those modern buildings which so often replaced the graceful, lovingly constructed old houses—quickly erected and as easily destroyed, lacking the closeness of shared experiences, the joy of caring.

Sighing, Ruby rested her gaze on the oak tree which grew like a sentinel outside her apartment building, its top branches reaching the level of their third-floor apartment, spreading gnarled and determined, sparse but aggressively promising. Her interest had been caught last fall when she noticed how the leaves had been replaced by a protective covering. She saw how tiny nubs formed along each deceptively bare branch, which all through the winter—despite cold, ice, snow, or brutal winds—had supported the buds, now swollen with impatience to leave although it was barely spring.

The day darkened, and Ruby was aware of her sister's reflection in the window. Phyllisia was in her customary pose, curled catlike, reading on the couch. A rush of resentment cleared away Ruby's starting tears. There she was, so involved in characters who could mean nothing in her life that nothing, no one else mattered to her. That was her sister's favorite pastime, her favorite position. It made no difference the time of day, the amount of work to be done, or if she, Ruby, was lonely. Phyllisia escaped all things by producing a book. Interrupting her invited a blank expression with a not-to-be mistaken annoyance curling the corners of her mouth.

Ruby was about to turn on Phyllisia when she spied a pair of broad shoulders through the branches of the tree, long legs striding toward the Robbinses' brownstone. Ruby knew who it was before she saw the strong brown neck, the bushy afro topping the well-formed head. Her resentment gave way to a breathless fluttering, sadness to a chatty nervousness. "I see your friend Marian is moving," she said. "I wonder where they're going?"

Phyllisia unwound herself and joined Ruby at the window. "So they're finally moving to the suburbs. Good riddance I say." She smirked. "I guess your friend Orlando is going to say his last good-bye."

"He is not *my* friend," Ruby informed her coldly. "I will never have anything to do with him again in my life."

Just then Orlando looked up and saw the two sisters at the window. He jerked his head around, quickened his pace to reach the brownstone. He ran up the steps two at a time and disappeared inside the swinging doors.

"Friend or not," Phyllisia said caustically, "you had better stop looking out of the window when that guy passes or one of these days his head will snap off his shoulders." She went back to her book but decided to paint an even more vivid picture. "Just think of that handsome black head rolling off his shoulders into the gutter just as a car is passing. Oh, gush!" She shuddered.

"Jackass!" Ruby spat the word at her sister, but she kept her eyes fixed on the swinging doors, waiting to see him come out. How long would it take him to say good-bye? *Not that I care,* she thought. *I used to like him but now I don't—I used to like him very much. But now I definitely don't—*

It had been well over a year since she and Orlando had spoken, since the night he had brought her home from Marian's party—only across the street—since he had almost kissed her and her father had bloodied his nose for his trouble. Since then he hadn't had the courage—not the courage—

The swinging door opened. Her heart leaped, pounded, shortening her breath. But it was only one of the moving men. She leaned her hot forehead against the cold windowpane, still waiting.

The day darkened, sharpening Phyllisia's reflection on the window. Ruby whirled around in sudden anger. "Can't you put that blasted book down and talk to me?"

Phyllisia started. "You want me to talk? What about?"

"Something! Anything!"

Phyllisia closed the book carefully over her finger and Ruby slapped it out of her hand. They stood glaring at each other.

"What in the devil are you reading about anyway?"

"About the Boxer Rebellion," Phyllisia said spitefully, knowing Ruby knew little and cared less about what she read. At sixteen, Phyllisia still had the soft contours of her early childhood. Her recently frizzed afro gave her the look of a young rebel—a young, round, baby-faced rebel.

"What's that about?" Ruby demanded.

"About how the British pushed the drug traffic down the throats of the Chinese during the—"

"Never mind. I don't want to know. I don't want to hear!" Then her mood changed completely. "Do you love me, Phyllisia?" she asked softly.

Wary, careful, hesitant, Phyllisia eased out her words. "Ye-es. What's that to talk about?"

"I just want to know." Ruby's voice sharpened again. "Do you love me?"

"I said yes, didn't I? Now can I go on reading?"

"No," Ruby shouted. Her scalp tingled with anger. She walked aggressively up to her sister. "No, I have to fix dinner and you have to help."

Annoyance curled the corner of Phyllisia's mouth but she responded quietly, carefully. "What do you want me to do?"

"Get in that kitchen and peel those dasheens and potatoes."

"Okay." Phyllisia backed away, kept backing away until she was out of Ruby's reach.

Phyllisia had walked only a few steps down the long hall when Ruby's anger suddenly vanished. "You don't have to go just because I told you," she called after her.

"I know," Phyllisia answered.

"What do you mean, you know?" Ruby charged down the hall. Phyllisia turned, and Ruby, seeing the fear in her sister's eyes along with her intention to defend herself, flushed guiltily. "Come on, go back to your book," she pleaded. "You don't have to help me."

"It's all right," Phyllisia resisted. "I'll peel the dasheens and potatoes. Is there anything else you want me to do while I'm in the kitchen?"

Her unaccustomed obedience hurt. "I didn't mean it,

Phyllisia." She caught her sister's hand. "You don't have to. Let's kiss and make up."

"There's nothing to make up about. I'm not vexed."

"Kiss me to prove it."

Wariness deepened in Phyllisia's eyes, then she leaned over and brushed her lips across her sister's cheek. But Ruby held Phyllisia's cheeks firmly and kissed her mouth. "Oh *stop* that stuff." Phyllisia pushed Ruby from her, wiped her mouth with the back of her hand, and marched down the long hall to the kitchen.

Fighting an insane desire to rush after her and pound her back with her fists, Ruby walked around the living room, looking at the doodads on the shelves, picking up specks from the carpet, rearranging doilies on the backs of the chairs. Then, remembering, she dashed back to the window. The van was gone, the windows of the brownstone dark, the swinging doors still.

Misery erupted within her, tears rushed down her cheeks. She bit her knuckles to still her sobs. There was nothing to cry about, nothing, nothing, nothing. The branches of the tree nodded, nodded, in the sultry breeze.

Oh God, that Phyllisia, so cold, so unaffectionate, so damn, damn saucy, so self-assured. She was glad that she was strong, that she could beat her, force her to do housework, change her clothes, all the things Phyllisia had always been fighting and kicking and screaming against. It seemed to Ruby that her sister had always been around kicking and fighting and screaming over one thing or the other—no—no—not always . . .

There had been a time when there was no Phyllisia . . . when there was only Daddy and Mother and me . . . I remember that time . . . yes, I remember . . . Mother and I used to go to the Blue Basin . . . that blue, Blue Basin, where the branches of the giant trees came together to cut out the sun . . . where wild birds sang and small animals came to drink and cool off in the coolness of the glen . . . where bright red and yellow and orange flowers splashed against the dark green of the surrounding bush, making the bush seem darker, myste-

rious . . . and where the waterfalls tumbling into the Blue Basin kept up that constant rhythm, adding to the mystery . . . I remember once when Mother and I, tired from a long walk on a hot day, went there to swim and play . . . I remember how she stripped naked and dived into the Basin, swimming down, down, down until she became so small it was as though she would melt into the bottom of that bottomless Basin . . . I remember thinking that she might fade forever . . . how afraid I was . . . how I screamed and screamed and screamed . . . how I cried and cried . . . on the bank of that Basin looking at her disappear before my eyes . . . but then she pulled herself back to life size again . . . how happy I was . . . how happy . . . then we played on the bank of the Blue Basin . . . Mother and me . . . we played and played . . . how lovely she was . . . naked, her body cool from the water . . . relaxed from being in the shade of the dell . . . and she undressed me and put me into the water . . . tried to teach me to swim . . . to kick my legs . . . to use my arms . . . how we played and laughed and were happy . . . just we two, naked and alone . . . Then Daddy found us . . . like a giant shadow that darkened the dell he towered over us . . . and in a voice that frightened the animals and silenced the birds singing in the trees: "Christ, Ramona, what a shameless thing to bathe naked so with a child. Is so you want to bring she up?" Mother laughed . . . she laughed up in his face . . . she laughed and laughed and pulled me to her breasts . . . her full breasts . . . laughed until his anger fled and that other look . . . that unsettling look of admiration . . . and love . . . and tenderness . . . Phyllisia had never seen him tender so . . . Phyllisia did not know he could be tender . . . but he could be . . . remarkably so . . . but then it had only been Mother, Daddy, and me . . . then one day there she was, "the baby" . . . no, Phyllisia never did know the joy of swimming alone with Mother in the Blue Basin. . . .

Ruby wrenched her mind back to the present as the image of their mother standing in the living room—this very living room—intruded. She and Phyllisia sitting on that red mohair couch, their mother before them, her breast bared and that ugly twisted map of scars where one of those lovely breasts had been gouged away to halt the spread of cancer.

And as the memories joined, a rush of affection overwhelmed her. They were so close, she and Phyllisia. They had shared so much, they had suffered so much together. Then why had she been so mean, so vicious to Phyllisia lately? Granted that Phyllisia was lazy. It was Ruby who had cared for and babied and spoiled her. Why, why did Ruby torment her so of late? Guilty, remorseful, Ruby left the window and hurried down the hall to the kitchen.

Phyllisia had already peeled away most of the vegetables in her haste to finish and get back to her book. "Look how you're wasting the food," Ruby cried. "Do you know how far I had to go to buy that dasheen?" The purplish yam was sold in Puerto Rican neighborhoods, none of which were near their house. But Phyllisia, glancing sideways, noticed that Ruby was "back to normal" and grinned impishly.

"Ruby, you must be a mind reader. How you know I longed for dasheen and buljol this day?" Ruby smiled, knowing the implied compliment was meant to flatter, but not really minding the slight deception. "You're just about the smartest sister a girl like me can have." Finished with the vegetables, Phyllisia put the knife down, went to Ruby, and kissed her cheeks. Then, before Ruby could respond, she walked out, leaving her to clear up the mess of peelings and get about her cooking.

Ruby enjoyed cooking—cooking and cleaning and preparing things to give pleasure. Still, she would have liked Phyllisia to stay, to keep her company. When Phyllisia chose, she could be such fun. Ruby liked company. Loud, lively, provocative company. She loved it when her father's friends came to the house, with their loud talk and louder laughter. But their visits were rare now that Daddy kept busier and busier. The house was silent now, lonely. Then she remembered she had to tell Daddy about Ernest, the boy who lived upstairs.

Daddy won't mind Ernest . . . he's such a Mama's

*boy . . . but smart . . . I can tell by the way he holds
his books . . . and is always dreaming . . . blinking
behind those silver-rimmed glasses . . . of course he's a
snob . . . but only because of his doting Mother . . . "I
tutor for money you know" . . . he had held his throat
when he said it . . . so frail . . . so delicate . . . "but I
like your eyes . . . I'll give you an hour of my time three
times a week . . . but only because of your eyes . . .
that is, if you are not an absolute dunce . . . I tell you I
just don't have patience with stupid people." No . . .
Daddy should not mind him . . . he's so . . . so unlike
Orlando. . . . Orlando . . . so big . . . so broad . . .
yet so afraid of Daddy . . . Daddy shouldn't have hit
him . . . he wasn't doing anything but saying good
night . . . Daddy should have believed me . . . he
knows I never lie . . . I never, never lie . . . after all, I
am eighteen. . . .*

The sound of her father's keys in the door interrupted
her thoughts, and washing her hands, she hurried up the
hall to greet him. But he had already gone into the living
room—on his afternoon inspection—and was standing,
hands on hips, glaring at Phyllisia. "Princess," he said
sarcastically. "You ain't get off your arse yet to help your
sister?"

"She did help." Ruby came to her sister's defense. "She
did everything I asked." Calvin Cathy, with his stern, no-
nonsense attitude, his rigidity, his old-fashioned notions,
inevitably clashed with Phyllisia, her languid laziness.
Neither had any intention of changing—Calvin, because
he felt righteous, and Phyllisia, because she kept her distance from him in the pages of books. As the buffer between them, Ruby was dedicated to keeping peace in the
house.

"It look like she ain't move since last week," he answered gruffly, staring at Phyllisia. Phyllisia lifted her
head, ready to get out of his reach if he moved toward
her. Instead, he walked out of the room and down the hall
to the kitchen, where he inspected the pots on the stove.

"Eh girl, you got buljol," he said appreciatively. The
dried codfish salad was his favorite meal. He allowed a

smile to light up his brown eyes—eyes the same color as hers yet unlike hers because they were unadorned with heavy eyebrows and thick lashes, but equally attractive because they contrasted sharply with his black skin.

"Will you stay for dinner?" She blushed with pleasure.

"Nuh, I busy tonight. But save some for me breakfast. And make some bakes if you have the time." Kneading the dough to fry for bakes was time-consuming, but he asked simply because he wanted to prolong her pleasure.

"Of course I have the time."

"Nun nuh. Sometime when you ain't have school. I'll eat it so." She didn't insist. "I'll make some more Saturday," she promised, searching through his eyes. His gaze slid from hers, embarrassed—he was always embarrassed at her open, probing gaze. He walked out of the kitchen and went to his room. The kitchen became empty suddenly, terribly empty. She already missed his bigness, his loudness, the blend of his cologne and cigarettes mixed with the faint smell of rum, which whelmed her senses, tantalized her with suggestions of half-remembered things. Why did he never show his tenderness: pull her hair, touch her hands, her shoulders—why did he never kiss her, talk of how pretty she was? He used to brag about her beauty—had never stopped bragging. But now—

Cutting tomatoes and onions, shredding the dried codfish for the buljol, she listened for the sounds of his moving about. He rarely remained in his room for more than a few minutes; never more than ten. He never rested. From ten in the morning when he wound himself up for the day, until he came home from his restaurant at three, sometimes four in the morning, he was always moving. These periodic daily check-ups on their safety—or behavior—were the only breaks he allowed himself from the grueling pace of his day. His three great worries were that his children were in danger or acting up or that his help was cheating him blind.

He was already at the door when Ruby, remembering about Ernest, ran to intercept him. "Daddy, I—I have this friend who lives upstairs coming to help me with my homework—starting after school tomorrow . . ."

He waited for her to finish. She fumbled with her words. "What's wrong with that?" he asked. "I ain't see nothing wrong with that." He waited to hear what she might add. She hesitated, added nothing. He went out. Ruby ran to the window and watched him get into his black Buick and drive away.

"I got this friend," Phyllisia mimicked. "Why didn't you tell him it was a boy and get it over with?"

"I didn't lie."

"You didn't lie." Phyllisia shook her head, smirking.

"Anyhow, he won't mind Ernest. Ernest is so frail and pale—and you know Daddy is worried about my school marks."

"Well, I'll tell you one thing." Phyllisia shook her head and bent over her book. "Better you than me."

2

Kaleidoscopic images danced on each page, and noticing that she was seeing one page over and over again, Ruby looked up to the top of the page, noticed that she was already on page thirty-seven and had not read one word of her homework. She turned back to page fifteen of the American history book and started over again. But no sooner had she come to the end of that page when a gust of wind shook the windows of the classroom and pulled her attention away from the book. How cold it was. How thick and gray the skies. It was going to snow. And yesterday had been such a lovely springlike day, a tricky day, teasing the buds to open. What would happen if it remained so cold and it snowed? What would happen to the buds?

"Good morning, Ruby." Ruby pulled her gaze away from the window with an effort. She looked up into Consuela Hernandez's dense brown eyes.

"Good morning, Consuela. How are you?"

"Very well, thank you. Ruby, I'm sorry about last night."

Ruby's eyes widened with concern. Last night? What was supposed to have happened last night? "I wanted to telephone as I had promised, but my father had company to dinner . . ."

"Oh." Ruby smiled in relief. She had forgotten the promise. In truth she had forgotten about Consuela. Frowning, she thought it was terrible to actually forget her only friend the moment she was out of sight. Now she gazed up at the tall, blond girl, whose charm and warm disposition had impressed her at the beginning of the year. "I understand," she said. "I was busy after I finished dinner—or I might have called you." Consuela went to her seat and Ruby, following her movements, thought, *How could I have forgotten? That will never do.*

Consuela and Ruby had found an answer for friendship in each other, Ruby's friends from last year having dropped her as an "Uncle Tom," and the Puerto Rican students resenting Consuela because of her reserve, her middle-class attitudes. Calvin had met Mr. and Mrs. Hernandez by telephone and they all approved of the friendship.

Students straggled into the classroom singly and in pairs. "You with the bedroom eyes, what are you dreaming about?" The suggestive quality in the voice, the leering of the boy's face brought Ruby to attention and she turned primly to her book. Ed Brooks, brown, pale, sickly looking, and he had the nerve to be fresh!

He sat next to her, and Giorgio, his Italian friend, with the shadowy beginning of a mustache, slipped into the seat on the other side of him. He chuckled and added his greetings. "Morning, gorgeous, luscious." Nasty, coarse— God, how she hated them!

She started reading again with determination. History was her most important subject. While math was the most difficult, the teacher in that class didn't matter to her. Miss O'Brien mattered. It mattered that she appeared well-versed, articulate, even brilliant in Miss O'Brien's class. She wanted those sea-green eyes to crinkle into hers in laughter, admiration. She wanted to hear her say . . .

Suddenly all of her senses were tuned to the person who had just entered. Ruby's eyes did not leave the book. Rather, they became fixed on the jumbled print. She was totally aware of the long, well-shaped legs in their knee-length socks, moving up the aisle with that arrogant grace that every teen-aged boy in Harlem tried to emulate. The tweed skirt brushed Ruby in passing, and she inhaled to breathe the subtle fragrance in which the girl walked.

Daphne, Daphne. Daphne of the smooth, tan skin. Daphne of the heavy, angry black eyebrows that were so fantastically right in combination with her gray eyes. Daphne of the thick, well-formed lips, the large white teeth. Feminine Daphne with her thick, crisply curly, black shoulder-length hair. Boyish Daphne with her thick neck, her colorful silk skirts, her tweeds.

Now she will settle her six-foot frame into her seat . . . push her bookbag carelessly to the back of her desk, cross her legs . . . pat her moccasin-shod feet in time with music . . . her inner music . . . now searching her bag, she will find her file, look at her nails . . . the long nails of the tapered fingers . . . Daphne, Daphne, Daphne.

Not wanting to look back to reaffirm her knowledge, her inner, secret intricate knowledge, Ruby nevertheless found her head turning, turning and was looking into those eyes, those eyes looking through her, deliberately not seeing her. She twisted her head as fear jumped to life in her bowels, sweat itched her underarms. She stared into her history book as the print turned once again to kaleidoscopic images.

The shuffling footsteps, the tap-tapping of the teacher's cane as she dragged herself toward the classroom distracted Ruby. Relieved, she concentrated on the slow, labored movements, and waited until the half-paralyzed body appeared in the doorway before leaving her seat and going to the woman.

Miss Gottlieb was a remarkably ugly woman, partly from her affliction and partly because she had never been beautiful. Her nose was thick and heavy with small purple veins crisscrossing them. Her pores were large. The lack of muscle control on the left side of her face dragged heavily on the right, distorting her already distorted features. But although her left side was dead, both of her eyes were alive—brilliant, black and beady, shining with hatred, which she directed at her students—most of whom were black and Puerto Rican.

Her good-morning greeting to them was a sneer that spread her ugliness far beyond her face to embrace the room. Then, saving her best for Ruby, who was patiently waiting to help her off with her coat, she snarled: "Must you stand there breathing down my neck?" As she fumbled with the clasp of her black Persian lamb coat, her cane fell. Helpless, she glared at Ruby.

Without looking into her face, Ruby unfastened the clasps of the coat, helped her out of the right sleeve, then gently removed the cold, dead hand from the left, held it tenderly as she handed it into the right hand. Then she picked up the cane, gave it to the teacher, and took the heavy coat to hang in the closet.

Ordinarily, this daily routine would have ended quietly. But as she was unlocking the closet door, she dropped the coat. Ruby waited until she had unlocked the closet before picking up the coat. When she had hung it up and was returning the key to Miss Gottlieb, the teacher snatched it from her and rasped, "Clumsy idiot. I guess you would like me to thank you for wiping the floor with my coat."

Miss Gottlieb's ungraciousness was so usual that Ruby no longer heard her. What she did hear was pale brown-skinned Ed Brooks saying behind his hand, "Ain't you tired of being an Uncle Tom?" And Giorgio added in a deep-throated chuckle:

"Man, she's an Uncle Tom's Uncle Tom."

"Man, ain't nothing I hate worse than a white folks' nigger."

Ruby kept her gaze on her book. She had stopped trying to explain that she was not really an Uncle Tom, nor was she obsequious. There were simply things she could not do: she could not sit and watch a helpless old woman struggle, no matter if the woman was white and regardless of how ugly she happened to be. Yet she did care what her classmates thought. She cared that her friends from last year were no longer friendly. She cared what Daphne thought. And she did not want to look. She did not want to want to look, but she found her head shifting, to gaze longingly at the disdainful head, the beautiful hands.

Ruby entered the American history class reluctant but eager. It would have taken a major catastrophe to keep her away. It was the only class she and Daphne had together besides home room. It was also the only class she enjoyed. Miss O'Brien was the reason. Miss O'Brien was a joy. Tall, gaunt, awkward in her movements, intense in her love of history, Miss O'Brien captivated her students —none more than Ruby. As the coltish teacher stretched her ungainly legs, starting her perpetual walk, encircling the room as she talked, every ear was attuned: every student followed her movements, hypnotized, sucked into the vortex of her exciting personality through the interest generated from her intense green eyes—every student, that is, except Daphne.

Daphne looked bored. She was staring out the window, seeming to be removed from the pull of the amazing teacher. Miss O'Brien ignored Daphne. But it was a game, a game that both played well—a game that always intrigued the other students.

"Now, Miss Duprey." Miss O'Brien started the game at the end of her lecture. "Let me see if you can sum up today's lesson for the class." Leaning against her desk, half smiling, half serious, she waited as Daphne languidly turned from the window.

"I have no idea what you want me to say, Miss O'Brien." The students tittered. Laughter jumped into the teacher's green eyes.

"Suppose we start with the year of emancipation for blacks in the United States."

"It would be impossible to say, Miss O'Brien, since that year has still to come."

"I'm only speaking in terms of my discussion, Miss Duprey. At least give me back a bit of the information that I spent so much time giving the class."

"Then you will be forcing me to become party—unwillingly—to myths, so many of which are woven into your so-called history books."

"What I am trying to do, Miss Duprey, is to make you aware of the substance of history as it is written in our so-called history books."

"But my interest lies in the substance of *truths*—outside of your history books, Miss O'Brien."

"I'm afraid that is not what you will be graded on, Miss Duprey."

"Oh, Miss O'Brien, you know that I have been forced to make an A on that accumulated dribble that is thrust down the throats of us poor students."

"Then, I beg you, Miss Duprey, why do you sit in my class and allow me to bore you with my dribble?"

"But, Miss O'Brien, *you* do not bore me." Eyes smiled into eyes, appreciating each other. "You have such a lovely voice, such a vibrant personality, and a most picturesque way of weaving those tales. It excites me."

Was there a double meaning in Daphne's words? Was it true what they said about Miss O'Brien—that she was a "dyke," a lesbian? It was hard to tell. Boys as well as girls flirted with the teacher and she flirted back—at least she seemed to. Then Ruby asked herself the question that always hovered in the back of her mind. Did those two love each other? They seemed to. They certainly seemed to . . .

"Miss Cathy, do you agree with Miss Duprey?"

Splashing around in her fluid thoughts, engulfed in sea-green laughter, Ruby panicked, gulped. "I—I suppose so," she whispered.

"You suppose what?" Miss O'Brien prodded in good humor.

"What—what she said."

"But Miss Duprey is in the habit of saying so many things." Miss O'Brien sighed. "May I ask on just which point you agree?" Ruby's mouth opened and closed, and Miss O'Brien added helpfully, "Suppose we go back to the date of emancipation?"

That certainly was concrete enough. Ruby stared blankly while searching for an answer. What had Daphne said? She did not remember. Sweat trickled down her

back, under her arms. Brown eyes begged green eyes not
to shame her. "Yes." Ruby swallowed hard.

"Yes—what?"

"What—what Miss Duprey said."

"I'll accept that." A gracious smile. The sea-green eyes
embraced her, forgave her, lightened her sentence of
stupidity. The students tittered. Brown eyes thanked
green eyes, but green eyes did not accept gratitude—
never accepted gratitude. Miss O'Brien turned abruptly.
"Now, let me see if there is one student in this room who
was kind enough to listen to *my* interpretation."

Snow had begun in the early afternoon; by evening it
had become a blizzard. Calvin did not come home for his
after-school inspection, and Ernest rang the bell
promptly at seven. He came with a scarf wrapped around
his neck, his hand on his chest, complaining. "Oh dear,
this weather is too much. It's enough to give one pneumonia."

"Did you get caught out in the snow?" Ruby asked.

"No, no indeed. Mother took one look outside this
morning and absolutely refused to let me go out. And you
know that when it's damp like this the dampness goes all
through the house, the hallways, the bones." He shuddered. "Oh well, I promised."

Ruby smiled. How could Calvin object to someone as
frail, as harmless as Ernest? "I wouldn't have come out for
anyone but you," Ernest affirmed as they sat at the
kitchen table, set up for work. "I want you to know that. It
must be your eyes. They reflect your soul. You know,
Ruby, you are a good human being. Intelligent too. Whatever your problem is, don't worry, we'll get to it."

Intelligent? She used to think she was intelligent.
When she had first come to this country she had been
smarter than most of the students in her class. But this
year—this year . . .

*Surely Miss O'Brien sees some intelligence in me . . .
I know she does . . . or she would not mock me the way
she does . . . but Daphne . . . Daphne wouldn't know
. . . how could she . . . she has only seen me fumbling*

*with words, confused, dumb . . . she probably thinks
I'm an Uncle Tom too . . .*

"Ruby!" A querulous wail from Ernest. "You are either
going to give me your attention or I'm leaving right now.
I hope you don't think I came here to talk to myself. I get
paid for tutoring you know."

His annoyance shamed her, forced her to listen, forced
her to pull her mind back from school, forced her to pry
her thoughts away from the snow-laden trees, from Phyllisia curled up in her do-nothing posture, reading. Ernest
loved math the way Miss O'Brien loved history—with
intensity. He could help her. And suddenly he blinked
into her eyes, threw his hands up in annoyance as though
he saw through her eyes the assembling of her thoughts,
the efforts to direct them to him, keep them on his words.

"It's just plain nonsense," he almost screamed. "Everyone tries to make mathematics a confusing problem or a
complex of confusing problems, when in reality it was
devised to *simplify* the world's problems. Where would
we be in terms of time, space, the totality of numbers if it
wasn't for . . ."

Ruby suddenly found herself interested, relaxed, and,
as the relaxation grew, the insurmountable barriers that
had been erected like so many doors in her mind began to
crumble. The promised hour flew. Ernest looked up, saw
the wall clock. It was past eight. "Oh dear, I overstayed
my time. Mother will be simply out of her . . ."

They both looked at the doorway at the same time.
Calvin had suddenly appeared there. "Daddy." Ruby
glowed from the excitement of the lesson. "This is Ernest,
the boy who—"

"Mr. Cathy, I'm certainly glad to meet *you.*" Ernest
interrupted with an exaggerated wave of his hand and an
appreciative blink at the tall, handsome man framing the
door. Calvin's face clouded. "I'm helping your—"

"Helping? Helping with what?" Calvin's voice, loud,
angry, bounced off the walls. Ernest shrank back into the
chair, his hands went to his chest to quiet his pounding
heart. He blinked as Calvin brushed roughly into the

kitchen, went to the refrigerator and opened it, shook the empty pot on the stove.

"What in hell he helping with?" Calvin asked Ruby. "You come home from school. You ain't cook. Sitting there holding hands talking and no food. What the hell he helping with, I ask you?"

Spinning around, he peered into Ernest's amazed face. "You live in the building?"

"Up—up—" The table shook and Ruby realized it was from Ernest's trembling. She stood up, pleading with her eyes. Calvin refused to look at her.

"Up? Up? Talk up, man. What the hell 'up' you mean?"

"I—I—"

"Ayayaiyayai. What that nuh? Half-grown man, holding hands, talking he helping. Helping what?"

Phyllisia appeared in the doorway. She must have heard the shouting and had come to help out, in her way. Only her way had never worked with Calvin. "Well, if you don't want anyone else to help her." she said, "why don't *you?* Do *you* know geometry, trigonometry, al—" Calvin's hand hit out, Phyllisia ducked; his hand hit the wall behind her. He roared in pain. Ernest jumped, scuttled up the hall. Calvin, nursing his hand, looked at the empty chair, looked around the kitchen, baffled. Finally he peered down the hall. Ernest had gone.

Phyllisia, the only one who saw Ernest leave, looked at her father indignantly. "Why did you treat him like that? Just because he was a boy?"

"Not because a boy. Because he was a funny boy."

Ruby sank down on the chair, put her head on the kitchen table, and sobbed. "He was helping me so much, Daddy. He was helping me."

"There are people who ain't funny you can get to help."

"Ernest is no funny boy," Phyllisia defended stoutly. "He's a mama's boy."

Torn between Phyllisia's explanation and Ruby's tears, Calvin tramped up the hall in his wet shoes. "Funny boy, mama boy. Same damn thing." He slammed the door as he left.

"Phyllisia, Phyllisia, what am I going to do now?"

"Thank God he didn't waste the little squirt," Phyllisia said, giggling helplessly as she remembered Ernest's rapid flight. "Ruby, Calvin is improving."

The next day after school Ruby waited on the stoop to apologize to Ernest. She had been unable to sleep all night and in school had been haunted by his quivering fear. "Ernest!" She ran to him as he approached the stoop. Seeing her coming, Ernest turned and darted in the other direction. She went upstairs, waited at the window for his return, then opened the door as she heard his light footsteps on the stairs. "Ernest, please—"

"Aawk!" He jumped back, blinked in terror, then measuring the distance between them, he scooted past her and up the stairs.

An hour later the bell rang. Ruby opened the door. Ernest's mother stood there, clutching her shawl. "What have you done to him? The poor boy is out of his mind with terror since . . ."

"My—my father—is just loud . . ."

"Loud indeed!" The tiny woman looked as though she was capable of taking on even a Calvin. "What a way to do, shout at people who are decent enough to offer their services. My son gets paid for tutoring, you know."

Ruby looked sadly after the woman as she walked up the stairs. Why were people hurt for nothing? She could never forgive Daddy this, never in all her life.

For the rest of the week her mind was a total blank in school, but her anger and resentment made a terrible change in the apartment. She refused to speak to her father, and if it mattered to him, it only showed in that he stopped speaking to Phyllisia too. Ignoring them both, he came in and went out of the house like a bull. The strain even told on Phyllisia, who closed her book several times to look for her and demand: "What's going on in this house anyway?"

There was no telling how long the situation might have gone on, but on Friday Phyllisia, crawling into bed around two in the morning, complained: "Oh God! That man is aggravating, yes? A little sore throat and he's in there bawling like a baby."

"Who?"

"Your father, that's who."

All of her anger and resentment was washed away in one surge of fear. She bounded out of the bed and ran into the next room where the big man lay tossing on the bed. "What's the matter, Daddy?"

"Ayayai, ohyoyoi, I sick, I sick, I sick." Fever burned in his red, teary eyes. "Oh God, Ruby, I sick. I ask that other one for water. She bring it and she gone." Ruby touched his brow, then drew away her hand from his head. "I near dead I tell you and all you two can do is sleep."

"Don't worry, Daddy, I'll take care of you." She kissed his hot brow and rearranged the bedclothes. She went into the bathroom and came back with an armful of remedies. It was touching, his hurt over Phyllisia's lack of concern.

She rubbed his chest with alcohol, and at the feel of her cool, competent hands, he managed an obsequious smile, a maudlin entreaty that she save his life. She felt his pulse, satisfying herself that he was not in danger. She applied Vicks on his chest and neck, and he fell asleep.

After calling his two friends, Cousin Frank and Mr. Charles, to tell them of his sickness, she sat by his bed all night. When he awoke during the night, she gave him juice, insisted he drink, straightened the crumpled bedclothes, helped him to the bathroom—like a cripple he put most of his weight on her shoulders—then tucked him in again. Once when she started to leave the room he uttered a moan that brought her rushing back to his side to comfort him. "I'm not leaving. I'll be right back. Now try to sleep." Thanking her with his eyes, he submitted weakly, going right off to sleep. Ruby smiled at the idea that such a tiny baby could be wrapped up in such a big man. And she felt overwhelmingly tender toward him.

But despite all Ruby's care, Calvin's temperature climbed. His lips cracked, heat radiated from his body, and a smell of sickness pervaded the room. Phyllisia made an appearance before going to bed. "How is he?" she asked.

"I don't know. His fever keeps climbing. I think I had better call an ambulance."

"An ambulance?" Phyllisia said doubtfully. "Did you give him aspirins?"

"I did."

"How many?"

"I gave him two last night and two—"

"That's not enough. Give him six."

"Six aspirins! Are you out of your mind?"

"Wake him, give him the aspirins," Phyllisia insisted. "That's what the ambulance man would do."

Ruby looked thoughtfully at her younger sister. She did not like her reasoning, but Phyllisia, with her head always in books, could bring proof to support her arguments. With the help of Phyllisia, she awoke Calvin, made him take the aspirins, which in his semiconscious state he gulped without protest. Still she was concerned.

"It seemed an awful lot, Phyllisia. I hope it won't hurt him."

"Hurt him?" Phyllisia scoffed.

"People die sometimes from taking too many pills, Phyllisia."

"Ch—upps." Phyllisia sucked her back teeth contemptuously. "Ruby, *ordinary* people die from taking too many pills. Your father is not ordinary." Then, at Ruby's startled look, she added, "But *you* are, so you had better get some sleep."

Phyllisia's words hung over the room. Not ordinary? Daddy, not ordinary? True, he was big, loud, cruel sometimes—but not ordinary?

Sleepy but afraid to sleep, she wondered if she had been responsible for a serious mistake. Afraid to leave him, she lay beside him, dozing fitfully, awakening at his every turn. She listened to his breathing, put her ear against his chest to hear his heartbeat, smoothed his brow, rubbed his chest. Then, unable to keep her eyes open, she fell asleep. The wetness of her dress awakened her. Feeling around, she realized that it was part of a general wetness. The quilt, the sheets, the pillows and the mattress were all soaking wet. It was as though the ceiling had poured down water while she slept. His temperature had broken.

She changed the bedclothes, pulled down his soaking merino to his waist, replaced the undershirt with the top of a new pair of pajamas she found in his drawer. He always wore the long, old-fashioned underwear, over which he pulled on pants on his way to and from the bathroom. She rubbed him down with alcohol, changed her own clothes, lay back down beside him, and promptly fell into a deep sleep. She opened her eyes, much later, to find them looking into his. Sitting up, she stretched, smiled, felt his forehead. "Your fever is gone. It broke last—"

"But what you doing in me bed?" He interrupted her. "If you sleepy, you got a bed." He was feeling better.

As the day wore on, he grew increasingly better and became increasingly more difficult. Ruby had to insist that she wash his face, that she rub him with alcohol. When she asked him to put on the bottom of his pajamas, he rebelled. He took off the top and threw it at her. "I ain't never wear pajamas in me life so fold them up and put them back." Ruby insisted that company might come. "I ain't care. Give me me merino." She put the pajamas back.

He slept most of the day. Getting up toward evening and seeing her still sitting next to his bed, he demanded: "But where the other one? She know I here—dying—she bring me one drink a water and she gone."

Ruby went into the dining room, where Phyllisia was writing her Sunday letter to her friend Edith. "Your father wants to see you," she said stiffly.

The corners of Phyllisia's mouth curled automatically. "What he want from me that you can't do better?" Nevertheless she went in to see him.

Ruby left them to themselves. Standing at the window, gazing at her tree, noticing the buds had not been deterred by the late-season blizzard, looking at the streets wet from the rapidly melting snow, she fought against her bitterness.

It was the same with Mother . . . I had cared and cared . . . learned to read her pulse rate . . . her temperature. I loved her . . . surrounded her with love . . . and the last night . . . it was Phyllisia she called . . . the last night . . . Phyllisia. . . .

Phyllisia came back. "That man. Evilness is what is keeping him alive, I tell you. You know all he wanted? To make sure I was in the house. Ruby, I level one cuff at his head."

"You didn't!" Ruby rushed down the hall and into her father's room. "Daddy, are you all right?"

"And what will happen to me in two seconds because you gone?" Phyllisia had been teasing. Ruby laughed, touched his forehead, felt his pulse. He gazed at her in unveiled irritation. Ignoring his expression, she bent and kissed his lips. He twisted away sharply. "There must be one thing in this house want doing, beside you sitting there playing nurse." She sighed, forgiving him his gruffness, but the moment she sat down he added: "And if you ain't leave me alone this minute I getting up and going to the place."

She left him alone.

Mr. Charles came to see him that evening. *"Hélas!"* he cried, seeing the big man in bed. "A little bug bring down the mighty oak. Look at Calvin, flat on his back. Timber!"

"But where's Frank?" Calvin complained. "How he know I sick and he ain't here?"

"You ain't got to worry about Frank. He coming. If not today, tomorrow."

"Tomorrow! Oh God, Charles, I here sick, sick like anything and me own cousin ain't come. I tell you I was dead, dead, dead."

"You ain't look so. You look in good shape—better than when I see you."

"Oh God, man!"

"And not only that. I pass by the restaurant and the place is still there, the same way as when you leave and doing damn good."

"Oho."

"Isso. I pass there today. You kill yourself working and . . ."

"It ain't work that bring me down, Charles. Is flu. Everybody get flu."

"If they resistance is low. I tell you long time you got to rest. You a man, not a machine." Ruby, arranging and rearranging things around the room, smiled her agreement with Mr. Charles. He reached up and caught her hand. "Me, if I had a pretty nurse so, I would be flat on me back—at least twice a week."

Calvin shook his head in exasperation. "Man, you ain't know what I been through. I tell you is she the bug. That girl ain't keep still one minute since I here. She doing this, she doing that—all day long."

Affectionately Ruby pushed Calvin back on his pillows. "Daddy's such a baby when he's sick, Mr. Charles."

"Babying me is what she call it."

"From where I sit you look like a real well-cared-for baby. A little big, but all the same . . ."

"There, you see." Ruby bent and swiftly kissed Calvin's lips. Calvin snapped his head away angrily. "Oh God, man! She always pulling and touching and lookin' in me eye so." He mimicked Ruby's searching gaze. "And this kissing, kissing, kissing. What it is about, Charles? I tell you the girl sick."

Charles laughed, and pulling Ruby to his lap, he cradled her head affectionately to his chest. "Ruby is like a kitten. She needs a lot of love and affection."

"Kitten? Is what you call it?" Calvin scoffed. "You mean cat, ain't you? Charles, you ever see a cat play with a mouse? They play, they play, they play, then all of a sudden they do they claws so!" He clawed his hands into the quilt. "They hold and hold and hold and they don't let go. Man—I tell you—I the mouse! Come tomorrow I getting the hell up and outta this house. If I get sick a next time, so help me God"—he crossed his index fingers and kissed them—"I staying in the place there, I ain't care if I must sleep on the counter!"

3

I could *run away . . . go far, far away . . . it will not matter . . . I did not know how much he hated me . . . he would only look for me for the show . . . grandstanding . . . and Phyllisia . . . she has her books . . . and I shall never have to go to school again . . . never again . . . never again to sit within four walls and force myself . . . to learn . . . to think of what I don't want to think. . . .*

Ed Brooks and Giorgio were laughing obscenely. She did not want to look. Ruby made sure her dress was pulled to her knees. She kept her vigil outside the window. It was a brilliant day, the sky blue, unblemished. The sun, emboldened, had hued the day in gold, gave it substance so that it resembled the amazingly golden days of April on the Island.

Unhappiness, nostalgia, sadness, loneliness conspired, forcing her thoughts away from classes and school. A longing to be on the roof of the highest building in New York—to communicate with the day, to feel a closeness to the Island that would give her direction. *What shall I do? What shall I do?* Then she turned.

The lasciviousness, the coarseness of their laughter—a

kind of grunting—made her curious, forced her to turn. She looked down at her desk and glanced sideways at the boys. They were playing with themselves! Both of them! Their pants were unzipped, their penises in their hands, and they were racing each other toward climax.

Ruby stiffened, twisted her head away. Petrified, she gazed blindly out the window. She had to get up, to leave. But to leave was to admit she had seen! Their grunting became more marked, the sensuousness more obvious. Didn't anyone else see, hear? Couldn't someone do something?

"Hey, man, leave that for your bedroom."

Daphne. Daphne had seen her distress and had come to the rescue. Her awe of the girl stiffened her body, infused a helplessness alien to her. Her breath quickened but she refused to turn.

"What you mean?" Ed Brooks asked.

"I said it. Zip up your pants." Her tone was, as usual, well modulated, intellectual.

"Girl, kiss my ass."

"Look, you mother." The tone had changed to match his in coarseness, overcome his toughness. Ruby turned in time to see Daphne snatch him by the collar and yank him off his seat. "I'm not saying it again. Put that thing away or I'll cut it off, put it in your mouth, and throw you out of the fucking window."

The pale face grew paler. Giorgio in the other seat had hurriedly zipped up his pants. Ed Brooks zipped up his pants too. Daphne walked back to her seat.

She did not look at Ruby, and Ruby, embarrassed, did not look at her. But she heard Consuela say, "Thank you, Daphne."

"That really is not my style," Daphne answered in her carefully molded accents. "I'm usually cool, calm, collected, poised, sophisticated, cultured, and refined." The class laughed, liking her. Ruby turned. She wanted to thank her now, but Daphne, arranging her books on the desk, kept her eyes turned from her—deliberately, Ruby thought—and the hot blood of embarrassment rose, burning her from her toes to the tip ends of her hair. Did

Daphne think that Ruby had wanted to sit there? Did she think her so unrefined?

All day the heat rose and receded from her cheeks, keeping her in a state of misery. Dragging herself from class to class, she wondered why she even bothered to remain in school. How could she stand the confusion of changing classes, the unsympathetic faces of classmates, the unadulterated boredom in the droning voices of unfeeling teachers. How could she stand it? Why did she stand it? She had the urge to scream out from behind her burning face, her feeling of guilt—to scream, to blame the events of the morning on all of them, on every one of them—to run out of school, leaving them to their own guilt. But she sat on, going from class to class, submerged in her misery, dutifully waiting for the day to end, that last bell to release her. And then what? Then home, home, home.

"It *is* a lovely day, Miss Cathy. The skies are blue, the sun is bright, but can I possibly interest you in what is going on in *this* room?" Ruby turned from the window, looked into Miss O'Brien's questioning eyes, and hers filled with tears. Miss O'Brien looked quickly away and went on with her teaching, keeping the curious stares of other students away from Ruby.

The teacher pulled her aside as she was leaving. Gently massaging the back of Ruby's neck, her shoulders, she drew her close. "Is there anything you want to tell me? If you do I'm interested. You did show so much promise at the start of the term that if there is anything I can do . . ."

The soothing hand touching, caring, feeling deeply down into where some pain, some unknown bruise waited for the balm of concern. And the concern was there, in the voice, the eyes, the pressure of the hands massaging, massaging. If only they would remain there forever. If only she could lay her head on Miss O'Brien's breast, keep the voice expressing the warmth, the knowledge of her need.

Looking up, Ruby saw Daphne standing by her seat, staring at them, her gray eyes almost black, impenetrable. Jealousy? Anger? Shaking her head that nothing was the matter, Ruby slipped away from the pressure of the strong, soothing fingers, missing them, needing them, feeling a strange emptiness.

All through the evening, the night, two pairs of eyes—one green, the other gray—haunted her. They haunted her daydreams, her dreams, manipulated her moods so that at one moment she was deliriously, senselessly, happy, her spirits light, floating wispy, cloudlike as on a breeze; the next, embarrassment, misery, pulled her down into a quagmire of depression, deadened her spirits, threatened her with oblivion, awakened her to the passivity of her existence.

In the morning she wondered why she had bothered to get up, to dress. Why take that subway ride to a place where she took up space and other people's time? Feeling as though she were doing penance, she lingered around the house long after Phyllisia had gone, fixed an elaborate breakfast, and set an even more elaborate table for her father, postponing her departure. Even on the subway she wavered. A movie, a walk through the park would be more pleasant. Yet she went, pulled by a need that she did not understand.

Late getting to class, she found Consuela helping Miss Gottlieb off with her coat. Consuela, delighted at seeing Ruby, gratefully moved to give over the odious task and return to her seat, but Miss Gottlieb held her back. "Stay here." Then, pivoting on her good leg, she faced Ruby. "Who and what do you think you are, coming in at this time when you know you have responsibilities? Let me tell you one thing: I can do without the likes of you."

Ruby stared at Miss Gottlieb. She had expected just this, and yet she found herself unable to move. How well she knew this woman, knew that all things mean and ugly were in her. Yet it did not prevent her heart from aching, her lungs from refusing air, or the feeling of sudden death which rushed over her. "Get to your seat. Get to your seat," Miss Gottlieb shouted. Ruby couldn't move.

A sudden guffaw from a student, an answering chuckle, also without humor, forced her to turn, to question the class with her eyes. The room fell into a pitying silence. She looked at Daphne. Daphne was buffing her nails with such intensity that Ruby knew she had seen far more deeply into the scene than the others.

Perhaps that was the reason that after school Ruby quickened her steps to catch Daphne as she saw her head high above the crowd, nearing the corner. She had started to run when she heard a call.

"Ruby!" She turned to see Consuela approaching. "You were not waiting for me?" Their situation had been reversed. Consuela usually waited for her after school while Ruby helped the crippled teacher.

"Yes, of course I was. I just saw someone."

"Oh, I thought you might be angry with me for helping Miss Gottlieb."

"No, I had no reason to be."

"I would not have helped her except she asked me to."

"I know." Daphne's head disappeared around the corner and an unexpressed hope fluttered, died in Ruby, leaving a strange depression. "Who else could she ask?" She consoled her friend. "I wasn't there."

It was true. She and Consuela had come from places, cultures where the old were revered, pampered, respected. Where they could do no wrong and the most impossible demands were carried out—or at least considered with deference.

"What could I do?" Consuela complained. "She is old."

"Yes," Ruby agreed. "She is old." Yet their classmates had not held it against Consuela today. They had accepted somehow that Consuela was different. But Ruby they considered one of them.

"I hate her," Consuela said with quiet passion. "She is ugly and her manners are so bad."

Ruby turned the thought of hating around in her mind. She thought of Miss Gottlieb's black, beady, hate-filled eyes, the balding head, the loose, dribbling lips. She thought of the useless rag-doll hand—soft to the touch, cool, already dead. "It certainly isn't easy to like her," she answered sympathetically.

4

In the weeks that followed, Miss Gottlieb did even less to deserve the pity that Ruby felt. The teacher's dislike rose in direct proportion to Ruby's former assistance to her. There was not one moment when Ruby was present that the teacher did not sneer at her and try to insult her. When she received their mid-term marks, Miss Gottlieb singled Ruby out of the entire class for a special slur. "It seems we have an absolute nincompoop on our hands," she snarled. "Miss Cathy, can you tell me how your people think they can get away with it?" The thick, wet lips trembled with the pleasure of snaring the perfect victim. "These parents who send their morons to school and expect *us* to do something with them. They know where those morons will end up. Where they always end up."

The students stared disgustedly at her. They had grown tired of her inner as well as outer ugliness. Her continuous attacks on Ruby, after her months of tireless dedication, had taken their toll on the whole class.

Ruby's marks *had* plummeted to unbelievable lows. Her father was upset. "You ain't in this country to shame me," he informed her. "Whatever in your head, get it out now. Is one thing to think about—getting into college.

You're going if I got to beat your tail in." Then, realizing how irrational all that sounded, he added: "I ain't care if you study all summer, all winter, for the next five years—you going—so you might as well finish now." He paced back and forth, from the living room to the hall, down the hall and back again, hardly noticing that she was not responding, not caring, not really listening to what he had to say. Phyllisia was the one who listened, who looked at him—following his movements as he took the long hall-way in a few strides—with a sort of wonder.

"I ain't understand how come you slow down so. Your mother was a brilliant woman. And I—I—I ain't train in school, but I ain't slow—never—not in me life." He stopped pacing to look at her as she sat on the couch, staring without expression into her folded hands. "You ain't come all the way to this country to end up no washerwoman nor clerk in a stinking office."

Then, after more pacing, he asked the difficult question: "What about that boy—the one call heself tutor or something?"

"He moved," Phyllisia answered spitefully.

"Moved, huh? Then who else?" No one answered, but suddenly aware of Phyllisia's accusing stare, he broke off his pacing and went out.

Miss O'Brien voiced her concern. That Friday as she was ending her lecture she looked into Ruby's eyes and said, "Miss Cathy, you do have lovely eyes. If their expressiveness were due to what I was saying I would be highly complimented. But I have the strange feeling you haven't heard a word."

"If you will please repeat the question, Miss O'Brien." *What had she been thinking about? It had seemed so important.*

"I don't recall asking a question, Miss Cathy," Miss O'Brien replied, stepping back. She reached for her pointer and accidentally knocked it to the floor. In a flush of guilt and confusion, Ruby rushed to the front of the room, picked up the pointer, and, turning it to the blunt end, handed it to the teacher. Miss O'Brien's exasperation flared again. "You are so charming, Miss Cathy. Why can't

I reach you? You were such a promising student. Won't
you let me help you?"

Miss O'Brien's sincerity brought unbidden tears, and
Ruby, returning to her seat, glanced at Daphne, hoping
that she did not think it was her fault. She had not intended to attract the teacher's attention, her sympathy.
But Daphne was deeply absorbed in her book and did not
look up.

It was strange how quickly the tall girl put distance
between herself and the rest of the students the moment
the final bell rang. Ruby, seeing Daphne's head above the
crowd, walked fast, forcing Consuela to walk faster as she
tried to overtake her. But by the time she said good-bye
to Consuela at the corner, Daphne had already disappeared. When Ruby arrived at the subway a train was
pulling out of the station.

Disappointed, Ruby allowed herself to be pushed onto
the following train, where she stood wedged in the midst
of the loudly chattering students. Why had she wanted to
reach Daphne? What had she wanted to say?

*I wanted her to know . . . to know . . . that Miss
O'Brien . . . What about Miss O'Brien? She is only our
teacher . . . that's all . . . I wanted her to be proud
of me . . . Miss O'Brien . . . Daphne? . . . Why
Daphne? She is so intelligent . . . I feel so stupid . . .
so stupid . . . I didn't used to be . . . I didn't . . . Oh
God! . . . What am I to do? I am like a desolate island in
a stormy sea.*

She liked that simile. A desolate island in a stormy sea.
She curled the sentence around in her mind, smiling. It
was her thought, her words. Only she could have created
them.

And then the smile froze. Her heart catapulted, for she
was looking at a head almost two cars away—a head iso-
lated because of its height, its exciting familiarity. The
head was bent to a book, the reader oblivious to the noise.

Ruby struggled through the crowded car, elbowed her
way through the thick of people. She crossed into the
next car, was almost halfway through, when the train
stopped and Daphne got off. Robot-like, Ruby got off too.

But Daphne had exited in front of the turnstile, and by the time the crowd had thinned, she was already gone. Ruby bounded up the stairs, reached the street. She spotted Daphne already one full block away, about to turn into a building. Ruby rushed to the building, only to find when she got there that Daphne was out of sight.

She entered the dimly lit place, listened for telltale sounds, heard only a creaking elevator whose indicator lights had long since been destroyed by vandals. Ruby searched the nameplates, found "Duprey, 4E." Her finger hesitated over the scratched bell, almost touched it, pulled back. It probably didn't ring anyhow. She went back out into the street and retraced her steps to the subway.

The moment the door slammed behind Calvin the next morning Ruby was up and dressing. Phyllisia opened one eye, and began complaining. "But Ruby, it's Saturday. What do you have to do this early?"

"I have to see someone."

"On a Saturday morning?"

Ruby rushed out without answering, and only when she actually found herself in the streets did she begin to doubt her intentions. Saturday was a morning that people stayed in bed. What if she was intruding where she was not wanted? Yet she quickened her steps, afraid of changing her mind. Turning the corner, Ruby bumped into someone. They side-stepped in the same direction at least three times before looking at each other.

"Ruby!"

"Orlando!" The meeting made them speechless. Then, to break the awkward silence, Orlando waved the container of milk he held in his hand.

"I just came from the store."

"I—I am taking a walk."

"Can—can I walk with you?"

"No—I'm afraid not. I—I want to be alone."

"Oh." He touched her hand. She drew away. "Well, anyway it's nice seeing you."

"But—you can always see me, Orlando. All you have to do is turn your head when I pass."

"I—I mean to talk to . . ."

"Then—you can say hello."

"And get another bloody nose? But I'd even take that chance if I had a little encouragement."

"Encouragement? I always look at you. And anyway why blame me if you're afraid of my father?"

His pleasant manner changed. "Afraid? Look, once a guy gets mauled by a lion, he gets mighty careful about touching the cub."

"Not if he's a real man."

"Even if he is a brave man. It's you who don't have courage, Ruby. You're old enough to tell your old man—"

"I have to go now." She cut him off abruptly.

"But you're still so beautiful," he said. "I think you're the most beauti—" She ran, trying to push his words out of her ears; him out of her mind. But as she rode downtown she could not help reflecting that he had grown even better-looking than she remembered. He seemed taller, thicker, and he had begun to grow a beard.

Ruby hurried off the bus and to the building she had gone into the day before, only to find that it was not easy to enter this morning—not easy at all.

Why did I come? What will I say? What do I want from her? I don't know . . . I don't know . . .

She walked to the next corner, stood uncertainly. Then she walked back, stood again in front of the house, looking in. She walked to the opposite corner and wondered if she should wait for a bus. She walked back to the building, moving aside to allow a drunken-looking couple to enter. Panicking at the thought of following them in, she started again toward the bus stop, and might have gone home this time if she had not noticed a man leering at her from a parked car.

Lifting her head proudly, she went into the building, walked through the dark, dark hallway to the elevator, and pushed the button. She waited with impatience as the car creaked painfully downward and the elevator door reluctantly opened. She entered, praying apprehensively as the tired car labored back up, and thanked God when it stopped on the fourth floor.

She followed the letters on the doors to apartment 4E. But when she reached the door, she was unable to ring the bell. "I am not bold," she muttered. "I am not bold at all." Back at the elevator she was reluctant to get in it again and suffer its age, aches, tiredness. She decided to take the stairs, but only went down two steps before she turned, ran back up and rang the apartment bell.

Waiting was agony. Seconds, minutes eased away while her heart pounded in her chest, her ears, her temples. She heard no sound and thought that perhaps it was because of the pounding in her body. She leaned against the door, and the stillness she heard within the apartment was a waiting stillness. She stared hard at the peep-hole, wondering if someone was standing there staring back at her, refusing to open simply because it was her standing there. She flattened herself against the wall.

What am I doing here? What am I doing here? I must be mad . . . mad to be here . . . at the door of a stranger . . . a stranger who obviously despises me . . . I must be mad . . .

Suspense, fright, her lack of purpose forced her away from the door. She walked quickly toward the stairs.

"The name is Ruby Cathy, isn't it?"

Ruby whirled around. The door had cracked open and the words were spoken through the unlit, chain-latched opening in the doorway.

"Ye—es." Her unsteady answer did not appear to satisfy the listener, and, after a pause, she stumbled on. "Your—your friend gave me your address." Her voice trailed off. She did not want to lie. She had not come to lie. But how tell that hostile, unseen presence that she had followed her home from school one day? What was her reason? "I—I—wanted to talk to you."

"Well fathers!" A soft exclamation. "Whatever friend can you mean? I have so few—and even my worst enemy knows better than to wake me up early on a Saturday morning." The tone—intellectual, carefully rounded, and pointed to embarrass—killed all hopes for understanding. And wasn't that the reason she had come?

"I—I—want—I—need . . ."

"These are not my office hours." The hostility deepened. Tears sprang into Ruby's eyes.

"Please, please," she sobbed softly. "I'm unhappy. I'm so unhappy."

"Stop that!" The voice was sharp, almost brutal. But the chain was lifted, the door opened. "Did you come to cry at my door and disturb my neighbors? Come in." And, as Ruby hesitated, "Don't stand there wetting my welcome mat. Come in, come in."

Daphne led her down a long, darkened hallway from where she could see the sun lighting the drawn shades of the living room. But Daphne's room struck her first. It was before the living room, at a corner where the hall turned sharply. Upon entering, Ruby noticed a second door in her room, closed off by heavy, wine-colored drapes, matching the drawn draperies at the window, which obviously led back into the L-shaped hall.

Daphne's room was bright, however, from overhead lights. It was a large room, furnished with a big mahogany desk and chair, a mahogany bureau, a ceiling-to-floor lamp, and a convertible couch-bed. The walls were lined with crammed bookcases.

Daphne sat down at the desk and motioned Ruby to the unmade bed. Ruby sat down primly on the edge, trying not to stare. Daphne was lovely. She wore shortie, see-through pajamas which revealed nothing more than that there was little softness about her. Her legs were well shaped, muscular; her shoulders broad, yet femininely rounded; her stomach flat and hard. Muscles accentuated her slim arms. Yet her hair, crispy-curly, tied with a string, hung to her shoulders, in a disarray Ruby found charming, softening the effect of her thick neck, her square jaw. Her feet were as well manicured as her long tapering fingers. Ruby had never seen such lovely feet. Struggling against showing her admiration, she settled for staring at Daphne's feet, and stared so intensely that Daphne's toes began to wiggle. This forced Ruby to raise her eyes,

slowly, slowly noticing, even as she did—self-consciously
—the smoothness of Daphne's taut, tan skin.

Then she was looking into the eyes, the gray eyes in
which the merest glint of humor surfaced—mocking,
waiting. The silence stretched out and Daphne's controlled face made clear her intention not to break it. Ruby
reached in her mind for words.

"I—I . . ." She swallowed. Finally she blurted: "You
don't like me, do you?"

Daphne's face relaxed in surprise. "As I live and
breathe!" she exclaimed softly. "Did you wake me up on a
Saturday morning to ask me that?" Reaching behind her
on the desk she took a ten-inch toothpick from an inkwell
and began digging around her large white teeth. Ruby
gazed fascinated. They were so large, so lovely.

"But you don't—do you?" What did it matter that her
words made little sense? At least it was a starting point.

"I don't believe it." Daphne blinked, deliberately. "But
since you ask, let's put it this way. I neither like nor dislike
you. That's the way I feel about most people. There are
some, however, that I don't dig. You—happen to be one of
them." Slipping slang into conversation was her way of
showing that it was not her natural speech pattern, that
she did it from choice. It seemed to matter to her that this
was understood.

"Why? Tell me why? What have I ever done?"

"Everything to make me dislike you. But, as I said, I am
not the disliking . . ."

"We have never even talked."

"I never talked to Hitler. I never talked to Wallace. I
never talked to Tshombe, and I certainly never talked to
Uncle Tom. . . ."

"So you think I'm an Uncle Tom too?"

"I guess you want me to be frank. So let me say I think
that you are worse than an Uncle Tom. At least Uncle
Toms tom to survive. But you bow and scrape with such
open-eyed sincerity. You are the most sincere person
about kissing . . ."

"I only help Miss Gottlieb because she is old and crippled."

"Most of those teachers are old and they are all damn cripples," Daphne said scornfully. "Their society made them that way and they don't need our help to stay that way."

"Miss Gottlieb is so helpless."

"And she needs *you* to help her? She made it clear that she doesn't. She treats you like dirt. She treats us *all* like dirt. That's part of her disease. She actually believes we *are* dirt."

"I don't think that you . . ."

"She needs us, yes. But not in the way you think. And we help her. We help her by just sitting in her classroom so that she can vent her hatred on us or else she'd go mad. Who else can she vent her hatred on?"

"You don't understand," Ruby insisted patiently. "I can't look at anyone and see them . . ."

"What would she have done if you had never left your island? Have you ever asked yourself that? Don't you think she would have found someone else? Don't you think that she has always found someone through the years whom she makes the target of all her lovely invectives?"

"Miss Gottlieb doesn't mean half the things she says. She says them be—"

"Because they are in her to say." It was obvious that Daphne, as in school, believed only in her own ideas. "And because they're in her she will be saying them until the other half of her dies, and she will be thinking them until the last pinpoint of light goes out in her brain.

"She and those like her hate us for being black, and they hate us because they need us. Who else can crippled outcasts like them teach? Decent schools will not have them. They sit there being paid to tell us all kinds of things against ourselves; then they hate us if we don't accept it as gospel.

"They build themselves like gods on our backs, destroy us so that we are little imitations of themselves. Only most of us can't hide our distortions with higher education. Their educational system only makes us fit for the ghettoes, where we end up destroying each other.

"You see? That's what being God is all about. So, if they are such gods, why do they need *your* help?"

Anger flushed Daphne's face, the hate she denied quivered there, blazed out of her eyes. "But you, you have to prove you are bigger, better. Virgin Mary. Pontius Pilate, Ju—"

"Stop it! Don't. Please don't. Can't you see, I am not an American! I cannot hate like you!"

Daphne's head snapped to attention. Her smoldering eyes cooled slowly, grew thoughtful, reflective. Perhaps in the labyrinth of her mind the thought was raised that she had ruled out options, jumped to conclusions for which there might be more than one answer. She leaned forward, pointing her finger.

But at that moment someone brushed the curtain. Ruby turned, caught a fleeting impression of a man: tall, white. The curtain, however, was only slightly drawn and it remained only an impression. She turned back, but the chance for communication had slipped by in that second. Daphne sat back in her chair, toothpick between her teeth, a sardonic expression on her face.

Silence settled between them, heavy, undefinable, and Ruby, searching through Daphne's eyes, found in them an agelessness, a network of complexities far beyond her abilities to cope with.

Is it possible to be in the same city . . . the same class . . . certainly the same age group . . . and be so far apart? If so, then why am I here? What strange force directed me here . . . when it was so hard . . . so terribly hard?

She stood up, defeat weighing heavy on her thighs. She remained by the bed, needing words, words that eluded her. She looked at Daphne, begging for help. But Daphne refused her, and Ruby stood in that heavy silence, looking into the face with the mocking eyes, the mocking smile that was forcing the meeting, the moment, into history. Then suddenly the silence was broken, the weight lifted.

"Damn, Daphne, you got to start preaching so early in the morning?"

Ruby knew it was Daphne's mother because of her

eyes. The woman stepped into the room past the heavy
curtains, her manner brisk and breezy. "Damn, can hear
you clear to the Bronx."

Apart from the eyes, the difference between them was
startling. Where Daphne was at least six feet tall, Mrs.
Duprey was possibly two or three inches over five. She
was tiny, from her well-formed features down to her feet
encased in spiked heels. She was fair, much fairer than
Daphne, and her hair was red, touched-up, although she
had a redhead's complexion. Where Daphne's skin was
smooth, poreless, Mrs. Duprey's was coarse with enlarged
pores, giving her the look of hard living rather than of
aging. But nowhere was the contrast so startling as in
their speech patterns.

"Hey kitten." Mrs. Duprey flashed Ruby a professional
smile. "You see what happens when you get up so damn
early? A goddamn early worm is always snatched by a
waiting bird. And the bird that sticks *its* beak out too early
has had it at the claws of some vulture."

"Mumsy, this is Ruby." Daphne smiled affectionately,
ignoring her mother's jibes. "She's in my class. We were
here discuss—"

"Yeah, I heard," Mrs. Duprey said sarcastically. Then to
Ruby: "I got to give it to you, baby. You sure know where
to come to get the bull."

Mrs. Duprey's need to tear through her daughter's arrogance gave Ruby a feeling of comfort. It rounded the
edge off her ignorance, redressed the balance in the
room, handed her an ease with which she could speak to
Daphne again.

"It *is* rather early," Daphne said, undaunted. "But we
will forgive her this time, won't we Mumsy?" She went to
her mother, hugged her roughly, kissed her, and teasingly ruffled the well-groomed hair.

Mrs. Duprey pushed Daphne away angrily, glared at
her, and patted her hair into place. "Anyhow," she said,
"I got to get my heels clicking. We underdevelopeds got
to serve our time."

"Mumsy works as a barmaid in a restaurant . . ."

"In the heart of Harlem," Mrs. Duprey supplied, her

voice edged in sarcasm. "The last stand of us high-yellers. Once upon a time we were all the craze, from one part of New York City to the other. But now, Black Is Beautiful. Those places that pay gets either blacks or whites. Either the afros or the straights. We in-betweeners are being eased out into the greasy spoons." She swayed out of the room, her high heels clicking.

"Mumsy used to be in show business, aiming for the big time," Daphne explained, a smile flitting across her face. Then, as though by common consent as the high heels clicked down the hall, they remained silent, listening. When the door slammed, Daphne yawned, continued. "She wanted to be a woman-libber but has to settle for being a liberated black. She's bitter." Stretching, she added, "And so you have met my family. They are fine people."

Nothing to answer. Nothing to add. Ruby walked to the door, stood, reluctant to open it, waiting. Waiting for Daphne to stop her. She touched the doorknob. "Daphne, do you think that Miss O'Brien is a cripple like the rest of the teachers in the system?"

She felt, rather than saw, the head jerk to attention. Daphne's tone was cool, cautious. "There are always rules that are proven by the exception—and these exceptions we should take advantage of." Ruby waited. Nothing more? "She is also a strong woman who can bend to pick up her own pointers."

Ruby opened the door, sifting Daphne's words for hidden meanings. It was too difficult. "I—I'm sorry I disturbed you. I—I just thought it would be nice to have a friend. I—am lonely."

"You-don't-know-what-the-word-lonely-means."

Daphne spoke slowly, holding Ruby at the door with her emphasis. "I happen to be the loneliest person in the world—with reason, to be sure. Do you see all those books? I have read them all—or almost. I am self-educated. That hardly attracts many friends. My father used to say that if you don't educate yourself, you won't get educated. And he was right. He started me reading when

I was five, sent me to private school when I was twelve, and then he died.

"Can you imagine what it is, sitting in classrooms with pink-faced teachers who cannot teach, knowing more than they can ever know? That-is-the-loneliest-trip-in-the-world."

"You taught yourself everything? Even math?"

"What came hard I was tutored for. My mother paid. She did it under duress, but she did it."

"You are hard on her."

"We are hard on each other," Daphne said brusquely. "I just happen to be bigger. But she can put down those size threes of hers and a hurricane can't budge her."

Ruby looked around the room. Phyllisia would be in heaven here. "You really read all of these books?"

"My father was a black nationalist. Books were his bible."

"And he died."

"Yes."

"My mother is dead."

"What did she die of?"

"Cancer."

"One can almost call that a noble disease."

"What did your father die of?"

Sudden agitation came over Daphne. She hammered her fist on her palm angrily. "Well," she said finally, "it wasn't noble, that's for sure." Then, pulling herself together, she added, "Let us just say he went out of here on a hummer."

Feeling the intensity of Daphne's anger, Ruby did not ask what she meant. Instead she announced, "I guess I'd better be going."

"Before you tell me why you came?" The sardonic smile back on her face, Daphne stretched out on the bed.

"I—I told you."

"I didn't hear."

"I—I wanted to be your friend."

"And so now you are leaving. You get me out of bed early on a Saturday morning to tell me what you can say any day in school? You are satisfied?" Ruby looked at the floor. "Do you think you have achieved what you came for—or have you changed your mind?"

"No—no, I haven't changed . . ."

"Then why are you leaving?"

"Because I . . . Because I . . ."

"Dear me, sirs. What trouble she goes through to make friends and how easily discouraged she becomes." Getting up from the bed, Daphne went to stand over Ruby, looking down as though from a great height. She held Ruby's chin, tilted her head back, kissed her full on the lips. Ruby gasped indignantly, her brown eyes wide, insulted.

Laughing, Daphne walked away, lay across the bed. "Good-bye, Bronzie. That is another trait I detected in you. Did anyone ever tell you what a great hypocrite you are?"

"Bronzie?" Ruby did not move. "Bronzie?"

"Yes. That's my private name for you. Bronzie. Brown, brown eyes, brown skin, brown hair—a perfect, natural bronze—and a hypocrite."

"Why would you say that? It's not true! I never lie!"

"I bet you don't. I just bet you don't. That's your great tragedy. You never think. You just say a lot of garbage that comes to mind and you call that truth. Good-bye. Go on—go out of that door. But don't forget—above all to thine own self be true, and it follows—et cetera et cetera. Go on home."

But now it was Daphne who was lying Ruby realized. Daphne who was telling her to go yet not allowing her to go. Her tone was angry, a demanding anger. She was challenging her, daring her to walk out of that door, daring her to say good-bye. And Ruby could not walk away, could not say those parting, never-to-be-spoken-again words.

Ruby walked over to the bed, sat next to Daphne, touched the broad shoulder. "Daphne?" Then she was in the strong arms, feeling the full strength of those arms. Her mouth was being kissed, and she responded eagerly to those full, blessedly full, lips. At last she had found herself, a likeness to herself, a response to her needs, her age, an answer to her loneliness.

"If you don't know what you are doing"—Daphne pushed her away, searched her eyes—"you had better stop and ask somebody."

"Daphne. Daphne. I have never had a nickname before. I love that name—Bronzie."

5

Love was green. Dark green, light green—the new light green of a world bursting with life. Love was blue. A pinkish blue, light blue, bright blue—midnight blue pinpointed by shimmering silver needles of light piercing the heart. Love was orange. A blinding orange pulling the world out of darkness, tinging the air with gold, plastering the sky with multiple streaks of brilliance; orange that opened the senses into exquisite, inexpressible joy. Love was gray, dark gray, smoky smoldering gray, the gray of Daphne's eyes. Love was red, the ceiling-to-floor lamp that glowed softly, guarding the curtained entrance of Daphne's room.

"Why does the light keep burning?"

"It is the protection of our privacy."

Love had many shapes. Diamond shaped, gigantic— the space between earth and sky, shrinking, shrinking into the persistent tear of happiness which clung to an eyelash. It was square, the dimension of a city, a block, a street, a house, a room, a bed. Love was round, the entire world growing smaller, smaller, as small as the protective circle of Daphne's arms.

Love was feeling—fluid as the waves of a sea, rippling,

rippling, rippling into the intensity of a cresting surf which broke into the gentle lapping waves to caress a shore. It was the eeriness of the continual glow from the lamp guarding their privacy.

Love was pride. Pride in a tall, perfect figure that towered over crowds, dominating the sidewalks where she walked, rooms that she entered, the world which she controlled: pride in walking beside her, matching long-legged strides, feeling her confidence like a torch. Love was looking at people, seeing them through another's eyes, looking them over, judging them and knowing she was right. But:

"Why did you look at *him* that way?"

"I was flirting."

"But you don't like *men.*"

"Love them. Admire them. Particularly admire tall, broad, black, handsome men."

Love was believing: "I am one hundred per, Bronzie. One hundred per nationalist, one hundred per intellectual, one hundred per lover.

"My lover?"

"Yes, if you want it that way."

"Yes, I want it that way."

Holding, touching, fondling, body intertwined with body, racing around the world on rays of brilliant color, roaring into eternity on cresting waves of violence, returning to tenderness, a gentle, lapping tenderness.

"You see? One hundred per." Smiling, exposing big, lovely white teeth brushed with vigor then dry-polished to shining perfection.

"I see." Smiling in wide-eyed admiration as Daphne's long, well-manicured fingers dug through layers and layers of scented satin lace and see-through lingerie to pull out a satin bikini, proof of the care that went into making her one hundred per. That was happiness.

There were moments of doubt, as when on their first morning back in school Daphne brushed by, took her seat and began the morning ritual of the manicure without one look, one gesture to signify there had been a change, a great change, in their lives. Looking at the aloof girl examining her nails Ruby yearned for some sign of recognition. Then Daphne, cleaning her front teeth slowly with her tongue, distorted her full lips and let one eyelid lower significantly. Happiness again.

Until the pale, brown Ed Brooks turned angrily, blocking her on the stairs. "So that's your speed? I knew something was wrong with you. Dykes is your thing." He put his hand to his forever swollen crotch. "You want to feel the real thing? Here, I'll let you feel it."

Hands grabbed him from behind, slapped him against the rail, pulled him by his neck, shook him, then let him stumble down the stairs. "You see, Bronzie. You make me lose my cool. I hate losing my cool. We must be careful."

And so they were careful. They didn't hold hands in school, seldom on the street on their way from school. But on the train as they rode uptown, they brushed body against body in exquisite contact. "I think I'll ride uptown now to pick up Mumsy." And so Daphne's routine changed slightly. Instead of going home she rode with Ruby, getting off and walking her to the corner before going on to the bar and grill where her mother worked.

Ruby kept her routine immaculately unchanged. Her life had suddenly become private—very, very private. She had secrets to keep, secrets from Phyllisia's uncaring flippancy, from her father's demanding suspicions. She knew he would not understand, would not try to understand her need for this girl. He never understood anything about her. And so to guard her life-and-death secret life in that room that the L hugged in its elbow, protected by the red floor-to-ceiling light, she kept her routine pure.

At least, she tried. And then one day Miss O'Brien came into class, angrily denouncing the murder of an American diplomat in South America. "This is one of the most shocking incidents that the world . . ."

"Is this diplomat related to you, Miss O'Brien?" Daphne demanded.

"No, he is not. But I cannot see what that has to do with it, Miss Duprey."

"Then I cannot see the reason for such agitation on your part, Miss O'Brien."

"Are you mad! Miss Duprey, the entire civilized world must be shocked by this outrage. The diplomatic cor—"

"Why, Miss O'Brien? Why do you think the civilized world must be more outraged by this murder than by the exploitation of the South Americans by Americans? Why must they be more outraged by the murder of this man than they are about their collective responsibility for what is happening to the peoples of South Africa, than what is happening in Indochina?"

"Does one responsibility necessarily negate another, Miss Duprey?" Miss O'Brien's eyes sparkled dangerously. "Does being concerned for the life of one man necessarily negate concern for the lives of others?"

"Your concern, your anger, Miss O'Brien, raises the question of priority . . ."

"Miss Duprey, I have never in my life met a more cynical—"

"May we go on with the history lesson, Miss O'Brien?"

The teacher's green eyes seemed to stand out in her head. The next moment she turned sharply away and began the lesson for the day.

Ruby stirred uncomfortably in her seat. *Why were they so angry? I have never seen them so . . . they always liked . . . enjoyed each other. But no . . . now . . . why was Miss O'Brien so very angry? Could she be jealous . . . of Daphne . . . and—*

"Miss Cathy!"

"Huh? What?" Miss O'Brien's eyes were boring into hers.

"As usual, Miss Cathy, you were not listening." She turned away in disgust. Students tittered. Ruby glanced at Daphne. The gray eyes looked through her, not knowing her, not remembering intimacies . . .

That afternoon Daphne did not wait after school. When Ruby came out, Daphne was almost at the corner. Ruby ran to catch her. "Ruby"—Consuela was hurrying toward her—"my mother called your father this weekend." Consuela walked with her, slowing her. "She is arranging dinner for you and your sister for Sunday afternoon."

"Sunday?" Ruby cried. "No! Tell her no!" Then, aware of her unspoken hostility, she smiled and said softly. "We —Phyllisia and I—have made other plans. Another time."

Ruby went to Daphne's instead of going home. She knew that Daphne would be waiting. She was. "What is it you want?" Daphne spoke curtly. "I don't have time, Ruby. I have to change and go to pick up Mumsy. We're going out to dinner."

It jarred her. "Ruby"?—not "Bronzie"? "What did I do, Daphne?" Tears were close to the surface. "Why do you treat me so . . . so . . . Is it Miss O'Brien?"

"Look Ruby, there is so much about me that you don't know—probably will never know. There is a hell of a lot about myself that throws *me*, so I don't expect *you* to be a Daphne Dupreyian overnight. But one thing you must know about me, I insist! That is, I cannot stand stupidity. It drives me mad! Do you understand? Mad!"

"You think I'm—stupid?" Shame rose like a wave to drown her. "You really think I am stupid?"

"You—my friend?" Daphne went on, not hearing . . . "I see people laughing at you and it does things to me. I either have to put them in the hospital or I have to put you in the grave. That is how mad I get! It goes against my better nature, my philosophy!

"And while we are at it, let me tell you that one of the overall philosophies that I live by—one that I don't intend to change if I live to be nine hundred—is that I shall always be cool, calm, collected, poised, sophisticated, cultured, refined, not to mention intelligent. Day by day it is difficult. Never have I realized how much, until today. Today I was ready to throw an innocent girl out of the window, because she laughed at a perfectly natural thing —a stupid response to a perfectly logical question."

"You really think I'm stupid?" Ruby repeated as her shame gave way to a deeper hurt.

"What in the hell else are you?" Daphne snapped, already losing her philosophical calm. "You don't listen. You don't read. You can't concentrate. That makes you almost retarded. Yet, you were not always that way. I would never have looked at you twice if you were. I would have closed you out of my mind."

"Daphne, you mean you would just let me go—never be with me again?"

"My God, Ruby, you are still not listening! You never listen. An honest-to-goodness moron makes more sense than you. What is the matter with you?"

How strange "Ruby" sounded on her lips, how punishing. Bronzie, Bronzie, Bronzie—that was the name that made sense. "You wouldn't let me come here? After all that we shared? You would turn away from me, forget me?"

Daphne stared in exasperation, then in fascination, the open wound of Ruby's terror disgusting, then softening her. Her body slumped as though rid of a weight. She reached out, touched Ruby's hair, her face, her lips, her neck. "It wouldn't be easy. No, it wouldn't be easy. But I would."

Suddenly she pulled Ruby roughly into her arms, held her. "Yes, I would. But what is the matter, Bronzie? What is bothering you? Doesn't being with me help? It should. You help *me*. Yes, you help me—so much. Can't I do something, anything?"

"I don't know. I really don't know. I haven't been able to pull myself together. I don't know."

"You must know. Who is to, if you don't? Do you or don't you feel that I can help?"

"I—I don't want to be without you."

"As I live and breathe! Bronzie, this is no time to play the romantic. I am serious."

"Do you want to help me, Daphne?"

"What do you think I am saying, Bronzie. I am saying that I want to help you because I don't want to *have* to give you up."

The face of Calvin suddenly intruded. Give up her privacy? Be open to his questions, his demands? Her secrets would turn to lies. Could she bear that? She had never lied to him. How to begin?

"Then I'd like you to help me."

"Let's give it a try—see what happens, huh?" Daphne's hands went to Ruby's neck, pulled her down, down on the couch that, when opened, would be used as their bed.

6

*This is the forest primeval. The murmuring pines
and the hemlocks,
Bearded with moss, and in garments green, indistinct
in the twilight,
Stand like Druids of eld, with voices sad and
prophetic,
Stand like harpers hoar, with beards that rest on their
bosoms.
Loud from its rocky caverns, the deep-voiced
neighboring ocean
Speaks, and in accents disconsolate answers the wail of
the forest.*

Stretched out on the converted bed, safe in the hook of Daphne's elbow, Ruby stared at the ceiling, red-hued from the lamp that guarded the doorway, staring at the images that leaped out of the pages to dance in the light of the ceiling, lulled by Daphne's rich, deep-throated voice as she recited her favorite poem, *Evangeline.* She sometimes drifted off to sleep only to be awakened by the pressure of the tightening elbow. Then Daphne handed her the book. "All right, now you read."

Reluctantly she took the book:

This is the forest primeval; but where are the hearts
*   that beneath it*
Leaped like the roe, when he hears in the woodland
*   the voice of the huntsman?*
Where is the thatch-roofed village, the home of
*   Acadian farmers,—*
Men whose lives glided on like rivers that water the
*   woodlands,*
Darkened by shadows of earth, but reflecting an image
*   of heaven?*
Waste are those pleasant farms, and the farmers
*   forever departed!*
Scattered like dust and leaves, when the mighty blasts
*   of October*
Seize them, and whirl them aloft, and sprinkle them
*   far o'er the ocean.*
Naught but tradition remains of the beautiful village
*   of Grand-Pré.*
Ye who believe in affection that hopes, and endures,
*   and is patient,*
Ye who believe in the beauty and strength of woman's
*   devotion,*
List to the mournful tradition, still sung by the pines
*   of the forest;*
List to a tale of love in Acadie, home of the happy.

"What a terrible tragedy, Daphne. Each time we read it . . ."

"All tragedies are terrible, Bronzie."

"True, but just think, all those beautiful people forced out of their villages."

"All people are beautiful, Bronzie, and all villages have customs and traditions. Do you have any idea how many people are forced out of their villages every year in South Africa?"

"But that's different!"

"Why? Because it's happening today and no one has yet written a lyrical poem describing the heartbreak and anguish? Do you have any idea what is going on in Vietnam —the type of uprooting, the devastation caused by B-52s, by defoliation—to the lives of millions of people? Bronzie, this bit about your being non-American is a moot one if you think—or rather non-think like the majority of Americans.

"Tragedy, my love, is *not* what happens in the lives of white people. It is what happens in the lives of people, places and things.

"Just think, Bronzie, of all the people who were uprooted from Africa and brought to the Americas. Never before has such a vast number of people been displaced. We know that hundreds of thousands of blacks perished in the middle passage. Yet millions of black people, with roots that inevitably lead back to Africa, people in the Americas, are indigenous to countries as far-flung as Nova Scotia and Brazil. Hell, in the United States, by a rough estimate, there are about thirty million—and what is the actual count of those living in Brazil?

"God, if epic poems and novels were to be written about our enforced trek around the world, the tales from the Bible to *Exodus* would be pale by comparison."

"And what of *their* wasted farms? The farmers forever departed? Do you realize that Africa is still underpopulated because of the massive, forced departure?"

That was Daphne's method: read, read, read everything. Compare everything. Discuss, discuss, discuss. Discuss until doubts were cleared.

"Daphne, I still don't understand."

"Those books on the shelves, Bronzie, are for reading. We will discuss this again when you have done more reading on it."

Reading with a mind to always disagree was not the reason most people read, Ruby knew. Yet her mind was opening, her interest forced. She researched, bought newspapers, magazines, read all sorts of material for just such a reason. Even when she agreed with Daphne she took an opposite position. When she was forced to back down, Daphne didn't mind as long as she had come prepared to defend herself.

Leaving Daphne, she always felt stimulated, happy. And they usually walked to the bus stop, discussing their weekends. "The weekends take forever to come and then rush by so quickly," Daphne complained. "We should be able to work later during the week and have the weekends just for us."

"I wish we could, but my father's creed is that Wickedness begins at Nine."

"You mean his lack of a creed?"

"Yes, I guess so. He pretends that it's Phyllisia being alone that troubles him out of his mind."

"Well, he certainly has power. We should refer to him as the *Omnipresent He*, spelled with letters capitalized and italicized. At any rate, he hasn't been giving you any trouble about staying late after school?"

"No. He's relieved that I'm getting on at school. He's praying there is still a chance that I might make college."

"Let's keep him happy." Daphne kissed Ruby as she boarded the bus. Keeping him happy meant that she get home, fix dinner, and be ready for bed by ten.

If only I can . . . if only I can keep him happy . . . stay as happy as I am . . . as long as I live. I shall never ask for another thing again . . . I am so content, so calm, so very, very, calm.

A few days later Ruby and Daphne were having a discussion about anatomy when Mrs. Duprey called from outside the curtain.

"Hey in there, isn't it time that Ruby went home?" They could still see daylight around the window drapes, but the clock on the desk said eight. They raced out, missed a bus, and had to wait fifteen minutes for the next one.

When Ruby opened the door of her apartment, she smelled something burning. A flickering brightness down the hall brought her racing to the kitchen, where she found Phyllisia, dishrag in hand, trying to fight a fire that had started in a pot on the stove and was blazing up the wall to the ceiling. Ruby rushed into the kitchen, grabbed a pot of water and threw it on the stove. One more potful and the fire sizzled, dying down. They ran into the hall, coughing from the smoke.

"My God, Phyllisia. How did you let this happen?" Immediately a picture of her sister curled on the couch while the pot of food smelled up the house formed in her mind.

"I was reading."

"If you must read and cook, why don't you read in the kitchen?"

Tight-lipped, Phyllisia turned from her, went around the house, opening windows before coming back to the kitchen to scrub down the blackened wall.

"Has Daddy been home?" Apprehensive, feeling betrayed, Ruby could not move from the doorway of the kitchen. Every little thing that happened in the house was a threat to her happiness, and this was no little thing.

"Twice." Ruby waited, but Phyllisia was giving no additional information.

"Maybe I should call and tell him I'm home?"

"Change your clothes and help me, nuh?" Phyllisia's anxiety flared out. "It's been an hour since he's been in. I won't tell him what time you came. I'll say it was just after he left."

Blackmail—but it had merit. She went to change.

They were almost finished when they heard the door open. "I smell smoke," he yelled from the door. They heard his heavy footsteps pounding down the hall. When he appeared in the doorway they were frantically attempting to remove the last trace of smoke. "Oh Go-od," he moaned loudly. "You burning me house down. You burning me house down. I leave the house one minute the next the place going up."

He walked into the kitchen, his hands in his back pockets, his astonishment a barrier against anger. "Next thing you know, all you will have me whole house down on me head. Oh God, oh God, oh God," he chanted, "they putting me out in the street."

Phyllisia grinned. She tried to pull her face into seriousness but the grin kept bursting out. She turned from him to hide her face. Nevertheless, he saw her body shaking, knew that it was with repressed laughter. He stared in surprised silence. "Is a joke? I work hard. Spend me money in this house. You bringing it down on me head and is a big joke?"

Abandoning all attempt to hold in her laughter, Phyllisia doubled up, holding her stomach. Ruby, standing on the stove looking down at her; Calvin in the doorway looking in at her. Both smiled. "If is a joke tell me. I want to laugh too," he said.

"But Daddy," Phyllisia gasped. "It's our house too. And if anybody had burned up, it would have been me."

He weighed whether to laugh, then said, roughly: "Well is lucky it ain't worse." He walked out afraid that she might take his unmistakable amusement for a sign of softness.

But the next morning he called Ruby into his room before she left for school. "You come home late from school yesterday?"

"Yes."

"What time?"

"It was almost seven."

"But why? Seven is too late."

"It was so light out, I didn't notice the time."

"Uhuh, it light nowadays. But the other one, she got so much air in she head, it ain't good to leave she long by sheself."

"Phyllisia is old enough to look out for herself. She's sixteen."

"It ain't that," Calvin murmured. "But look what happen last night. I bet anything she was in parlor reading she tail off and trying to cook at one and the same time."

"She won't do that again."

"I ain't know about that."

"That girl you stop at every day. . . ." Ruby's heart fluttered. She stilled an urge to walk from him, to refuse to listen to his instructions. "How come she never here?"

"She has other things to do. After all, Daddy, she *is* doing me a favor."

He searched through her eyes. Ruby sensed his bind.

He had been pleased with her progress in school. Nevertheless, he felt his authority slipping. He had often accused her, but he had always trusted her. Now she deliberately closed her eyes to him. Closed herself so that he could not read that she no longer needed the crumbs of affection for which she used to beg. She no longer needed him to remind her—as he once did—of her beauty, of his love—all those things from which he had shied in such obvious embarrassment. But now that her longings were not there open to his inspection, rather than being relieved, his suspicions had been aroused.

How well she knew him! How strange this delicate approach from such a demanding person. "But—every day, every day so? If it must be—so be it—but it seems to me she can come to your house—once in a while."

"I'm not the only one she helps, Daddy. It wouldn't be fair if everyone asked her to visit their homes." She stared at him and he stared back, doubting.

"Where she live?"

"I don't know. We work at the—different libraries. Depending on the subject."

"Ain't she got a mother?"

"Yes."

"Where the mother work?"

"I don't know. We are not on personal terms."

"Oho." Suspicion flared. "Look—you learning good, they tell me in school." He walked a delicate balance. "I ain't want that to stop. But is normal I know where you are—who you with. Let she mother call me, nuh? Get she mother number. Ask sheself to call. I ain't an unreasoning man."

When she left him, she felt tired. A courtroom trial could not have been harder. She had lied. It was hard to lie, but how else could she make her world secure? Lying created problems. It depended on others telling lies too. The first person to approach was Mrs. Duprey.

"So, you want me to call your old man to tell him that Daphne and you do your schoolwork in libraries?" Mrs. Duprey's attitude had never invited closeness, but now she was at her caustic best. "Why can't you tell him your-self?"

They were eating at a table in the rear of the bar and grill where she worked, not five blocks away from Calvin's restaurant. They were so close that Daphne avoided meeting him by taking a cab whenever Ruby came to the bar.

"I did," Ruby confessed. "But he has a thing about talking to parents. He wants to talk to you."

"Why can't my enlightened daughter tell him?" Mrs. Duprey's sarcasm was cutting. "He doesn't know her voice from that of a Forty-second Street whore."

"Oh come on, Mumsy, why make a big deal? Telling it as it is has never been one of your finer traits."

"Daphne, daughter, I lie when *I* want to—not when I'm asked. Dig it? I'm grown. I don't *have* to lie to a living soul. You can come on just as strong as I can—stronger, according to all that bull you throw in the house. I got to listen to that and then tell a lie to keep it going. Ain't that a bitch?"

"Mumsy love—" Daphne, unruffled, held her mother's face, and kissed her "—how can you refuse us one small favor?" Daphne was at her charming best. "Bronzie's father is one of those strict, puritanical Catholics—quick with his hands but slow upstairs. Meeting him is bound to slow our progress."

"That I can believe." Mrs. Duprey had many levels of sarcasm. "Well, let me tell you . . ."

A man shoved himself between them, interrupting. He was carrying a television set and talked in an earnest, low tone. "Let you have this for fifty."

"Sonny, I got a television in every room except my bathroom and my daughter's bedroom, and she would hand me my head if I put one more in."

"Twenty dollars. I got to have the money."

"Not if it's for free," Mrs. Duprey snapped.

"I'll take it at twenty." A short, fat, freckled woman waddled up and seated herself at their table, handing the man twenty dollars. "Just put it in that corner."

"Hey Aggie!" Daphne's mother greeted the woman,

but Daphne, on seeing her, shook her head in disgust and walked to the end of the bar, muttering.

"Coming to this place is like going to a bazaar."

"Don't get up on my account, Daffy baby." The woman laughed good-humoredly. "I ain't gonna be but one second."

"You still paying Daphne mind, Agnes?" Mrs. Duprey took a pad from her pocket and wrote some numbers on it before tearing off the slip and handing it to the woman. "It's about time she got used to the idea that dirty money pays for her expensive tastes."

"You would be a rich woman if you banked all your money," Daphne said loftily.

"But I don't!" Mrs. Duprey snapped, making her tone vulgar for contrast. "Somebody in the family has to take chances. Your father ain't left a penny for insurance."

"But playing numbers is so—so . . ."

"There's only room for *one* lady in this family," Mrs. Duprey said.

"There you two go again." Agnes laughed. "Don't pay them no mind." She smiled at Ruby. "Those two been at it since Daphne was born, practically. That girl was born ready to take off. She ain't never been young."

It was true. Ruby had seen a picture of Daphne as a little girl on her mother's dresser. She looked exactly the way she looked now except that her hair had been in long curls. The same eyes stared haughtily out on the world, the same charming arrogance in the Daphne-esque pose, already formed in the small body.

"But it was a shame her old man dying so sudden. He ain't even have time to think of insurance." The woman got heavily to her feet, shaking her head. "And such a fine-looking cat." She waddled away.

Daphne's agitation and hostility had become more evident as the woman spoke, and Mrs. Duprey, sensing it, leaned over to Ruby and whispered: "You'd think Daf was accountable for my sins. She would have a fit if she knew I bought six Sweepstakes tickets."

"What did you say, Mumsy?"

"I said that because of my daughter I'm willing to sin.

Now what's that you want me to tell the dear Mr. Cathy? Write his number down on this sinful pad and I'll give him a buzz."

"Aren't you leaving with us?"

"No. I got a heavy tonight." She winked. "Don't worry about your Mr. Cathy, daughter dear. Your mother will come through. You know she's one hundred per."

7

Miss O'Brien was discussing slogans which she said had far-reaching consequences in the life of man. She quoted Patrick Henry: "'Give me Liberty or give me Death.' This is as fundamental to the concept of freedom as the words 'Liberty, Equality, and Fraternity,' born out of the struggle in the French Revolution. It symbolized the dawn of an era, the end of an epoch."

"But at that time, Miss O'Brien"—Ruby rose, choosing her words carefully, controlling her quavering voice—"after all, Patrick Henry was a Southerner who gave no thought of freedom for the tens of thousands of slaves in America. Likewise, France was fighting to stifle all liberty for blacks in her Caribbean possessions, even during the French Revolution."

Miss O'Brien's eyebrows shot upward, her eyes shot to Daphne. Then her face reddened. "True," she said, slowly, "but these were ideas whose time had come. Regardless of the contradictions at the time, the words 'Liberty, Equality, Fraternity' certainly heralded the birth of a new period, the Revolutionary period, which continues today. Wouldn't you say so, Miss Cathy?"

On her way out, Miss O'Brien stopped her at the door.

"I can't tell you how happy I am that you are taking an interest in class again. Your facts might be a bit distorted, but the important thing is that you are with us again."

Brushing past on her way out, Daphne gave no sign that she had heard. Miss O'Brien kept her gaze fixed on Ruby. Yet Ruby felt a current—active as an electric shock —pass through her as it went from one to the other.

She was deeply silent on the way home, distressed. "Whatever in the world is the matter, Bronzie? Did your nasty neighbor try to get next to you again?"

Daphne was referring to Ed Brooks.

Ruby shook her head, decided not to answer. She was surprised to hear herself ask: "Daphne, why did Miss O'Brien look like that when I spoke in class today?" The petulance in her voice surprised her even more. Jealous? Had she reason? Why?

Then it suddenly occurred to her that the person she admired most outside of Daphne was Miss O'Brien.

"As I live and breathe!" Daphne's startled eyes searched hers. "Really Ruby, I give you so much credit for near perfection that it devastates me when you act so sickeningly ordinary." The punishment of calling her "Ruby" really hurt, and so she did not ask Daphne the next logical question: Why such anger?

The need to understand Daphne overpowered Ruby. The mystery that surrounded Daphne seemed a constant threat to their relationship, but she was so close-mouthed, so hostile when questions invaded her privacy. Overawed, Ruby tried hard to respect that privacy. Only now and then she found openings when she dared to question her.

An opportunity to ask Daphne about her father's death came one day as they were walking home through the park. Daphne was reciting Hamlet's soliloquy:

"To be or not to be. That is the question. Whether 'tis nobler in the mind to die, and in dying . . ."

"Daphne, what did you mean when you said that dying of cancer was a noble way of dying?" Ruby felt that the wide open space of the blossoming park was more conducive to talking about death than the intimacy of Daphne's book-filled, memory-packed room.

"Did I say that? Well, if I did I must have meant in the sense that in dying of cancer, the entire body puts up such a tremendous struggle. When it finally gives up, it's because it's used up—it simply can't go on."

"Then suicide is not noble?"

"If someone wants to die, why shouldn't they? People ought to be able to choose the way they want to go."

"Then your father—didn't kill himself?"

"My father? Of course not!"

"You said his death was ignoble."

"Did I? If I did, I must have been in one of my Shakespearean moods. My father went out of this world on a hummer."

"What's a hummer?"

Daphne's nostrils flared. The anger, the unrest, the intensity which always occurred at the mention of her father's death fought for the upper hand.

They had come to a crossing in the park, and waited for the traffic whizzing by to stop. Daphne, leaning against a tree, stared across the traffic lane at a drunk wavering on his feet, emptying the final drop of wine from a half-pint bottle. The man, unkempt, unshaven, unaccountable, had somehow found his way up from the lower Bowery and, from the trouble he was having keeping on his feet, didn't have the strength to make it back.

"A hummer?" Daphne repeated the words, not taking her eyes off the drunk. "A hummer is a fluke—a stupid, unnecessary accident that has nothing to do with anything a person is about.

"You see, my father was a great man, Bronzie. A revolutionary, a nationalist. He had been in every movement in the United States from Garvey to Malcolm X and Martin Luther King. He was only a kid when Garvey was deported, but he remembered his father crying. . . ."

The drunk sat down wearily on the bank across the lane, peering through bleary eyes at the passing cars.

"He was a member of the Young Communist League. He was never afraid to learn, to talk. And he never saw that nationalism was a contradiction to Marxism—which, of course, meant he was always in direct contradiction with the white Marxists. They called him racist.

"But he learned from them. It was by being around the white progressive intellectuals that he came to understand that culture begins at least twenty years before a child is born. He was self-educated and he insisted my education begin in the cradle. He was passionate; his self-education and passion left him wide open to get his head split by the cops on any American street."

"Is that how he died?"

Daphne became more agitated, angry. "That would have been the noble way."

The drunk struggled to his feet. He lurched into the lane in front of an oncoming car. A screech of brakes. Too late. He went up in the air. He landed on the hood of the car then slid off into the street.

Ruby heard the screeching of brakes, the raising of voices. Crowds gathered suddenly, swelling around her. She found herself on her knees beside the unconscious man. His leg had been ripped open and she was tearing the dirty cloth of his pants, trying to pull the torn flesh together to stem the spurting blood. Voices—jumbled, hysterical . . .

"I didn't see him. He stepped out of nowhere—I didn't see him!" "Get an ambulance." "Where's the phone?" "Find the police!"

A policeman materialized at her side. "You know this person, Miss?" Ruby shook her head. No. "Don't move him! Don't move him."

Ruby looked around for Daphne—couldn't see her. She looked down at the blood seeping through her stained fingers, and tightened her grip on the wounded flesh. "What are you doing?"

"Stopping the bleeding." She answered the stranger in a daze. How did she know if she was doing the right thing? How had she got out here? What indeed was she doing?

The man's pale white face under his shaggy beard was lined with dirt. His mouth foamed at the corners. Wine scented his breath, stale wine stank out of his pores. The sharp smell of urine permeated his clothes. She looked around, unable now to let go. She looked up. Daphne! Stricken face—fright-filled eyes—standing by her side—not speaking—not looking at the man—only at her—standing there only on Ruby's account.

Finally, the sound of sirens, the parting crowd, the white-coated attendant. "How's it going?" She let go. The bleeding had stopped. "Good for you, the bleeding's stopped. Bring the stretcher." And after what seemed an interminable time, she was walking again beside Daphne.

"Oh God, Daphne, that poor . . ."

"For God's sake, let's get somewhere to wash your hands." Ruby walked behind Daphne to a fountain. It was too small. She followed Daphne to the edge of a lake and leaned over, rinsing, rinsing, rinsing off the blood that had become sticky. And then Daphne vomited.

They took a bus the rest of the way home. Daphne collapsed the moment they arrived. "Call Mumsy. Tell her I can't pick her up." Then she closed her eyes.

Daphne's skin was of an olive smoothness that never changed color. Now it changed in texture somehow, became waxlike. And when life flowed back into her it was not in her skin but in her eyes. They became dark pools of wonder. "All that blood! Bronzie, I can't stand blood!"

Ruby, strangely exhilarated by her experience, was even more excited by Daphne's sudden helplessness. How odd to hear Daphne admit to a weakness. She brought cold towels for her head, alcohol to rub and massage her shoulders, her back, her feet. "Should I make you some soup?"

"No, I don't want anything."

How terribly young she seemed. At the moment she appeared to be even younger than Phyllisia. How old was she? That was another subject they skirted. Daphne looked older than the other students in class. But she was taller, more sophisticated. She could not be older—unless she had at one time been ill. She was too smart. Ruby did not dare bring up the subject now. Daphne reached up to her helplessly.

"Oh Bronzie, if you had been hit!" She pulled Ruby down, cradling her head to her chest, reversing the roles they had been assuming. "I could not have stood it." Listening to her pounding heart, Ruby had to fight nursing her. She remained cradled, loving it, responding.

"I would not have been hurt. That poor man . . ."

"He was not a poor man. He was a drunk, a wino." With the return of her assertiveness, she became again, suddenly, Daphne. "When that man's wine told him that he was the equal of the combined power of gasoline, steel and ego, he had decided he must die. He had been committing suicide for years. Whether he dies from this accident, or ten years from now from rotting away, he has already decided he wants to go. And to think you risked your life . . ."

"I didn't risk my life!"

"What do you call running out in front of those cars?"

"I didn't think . . ."

"You didn't think. You never think! Suddenly you decide you are Superwoman!"

"No, I don't agree. I reacted, true. But I must have instinctively judged the distance of the next car. I am certain that I knew I would reach him. Just as somehow I knew I could help him—perhaps save him."

Later they lay side by side, Ruby in the crook of Daphne's elbow, staring at the red light near the curtained door, reluctant to get up, both listening to their thoughts, silently listening to their thoughts. Finally Daphne said, "Bronzie, you are a strange girl."

"Why strange?"

"Just what you did out there today. It doesn't matter if it was reaction or actually thought out, most people could not, would not, react that way, and if they thought about it, it would be to decide not to be involved. I—I would not think his life was worth mine. My father thought the same way. No one was important to him if they were not important to a cause. And he felt that to be important one must control one's emotions—guide one's instincts. He had to decide many times whether to put his life on the line, whether to get his head beaten in, whether to be thrown in jail—where he might easily be killed by a cracker guard—whether he should submit to being jugged by an electric cattle prodder—all to protect some leader whose life might have been more important than his. He had to have complete control to do that."

"How did he die, Daphne?"

"He slipped on a banana peel on Lenox Avenue and fractured his skull."

"Oh no!"

"Oh yes. Care, he used to say, was the answer to a man's controlled instincts. Then he steps on a piece of the *Daily News*, there's a banana peel beneath it. I was with him. I saw the papers strewn all around the sidewalk. I walked around them because he had cautioned me. The word "care" meant life and death to him, and to me, because I was important—a cause—the future. I walked around but he stepped on them.

"A group of men were at the corner. They laughed—it was so funny the way he looked when he took his pratfall. He got up, laughed with them, took me home and put me to bed. He went to bed. The next morning he didn't get up."

"How horrible! How painful!"

Ruby lay, not daring to move, listening to the anger pulsing through the tense body, hearing the innocent laughter of men. "I cannot forgive him, Bronzie. If a person must go it should never be on a hummer. Bronzie, if a car had hit you for running out in that street to help a worthless drunk, that would have been leaving this world on a hummer."

She did not agree, but what was the use? Would she ever understand a person as complex as Daphne? "And you would not have forgiven me, Daphne? Not ever?"

Daphne's arms tightened around her. "It would make me unhappy, Ruby. I would remember that moment the rest of my life. And nothing could ever convince me that you hadn't gone out on a hummer."

8

Ruby opened her eyes to the red circle of light on the ceiling and knew that she hovered on the brink of disaster. Her eyes found the clock. Two A.M. She started to get up. The arm around her tightened, folding her into a drowsy intimacy. Daphne had had a difficult day. She had shared the day, why not the night? Ignoring the pinprick of conscience pulling at her, she succumbed to the drug of sleep.

But it was the prodding of conscience which finally woke her at the even more disastrous hour of seven that morning. The sun, already brightening the drapes, reduced the mystery of the red light to mockery. She jumped out of bed, dressed, and was on her way to the bus before Daphne had opened her eyes.

At seven-thirty she was slipping into her apartment, frightened. Had it been any other day but Saturday she might have made it to bed, or be walking about the house before he got up. But Saturday was his early day at the restaurant. Eight o'clock he would be on his way to their room to wake her, to give her money and instructions for the week's shopping. If only . . . if only . . . if only . . .

She took off her shoes at the door, tiptoed down the hall, quietly. She stopped, turned, and there he was, framing the living-room door, his eyes bloodshot, his face as grim as death. Her first instinct was to relax completely, fall on the floor, faint or pretend unconsciousness.

But her weakened knees refused to collapse. She leaned against the wall. What could she do? What terrible act could she put on to change his anger to fear?

"Come, come." Hypnotized by his calmness, his soft-spoken words which belied the anger in his eyes, she walked toward him, her shoes still in her hands. Phyllisia sat huddled on the couch. This surprised her. What was Phyllisia doing awake at this hour on a Saturday? "Is so it does go," he was saying. "I give you me trust and is so you does give it back." The calm voice forced her attention and she stared into his commanding eyes.

"Every day, every day, me mind tell me, it ain't right that the girl stay out every day from school. And every day, every day, I tell meself, she is me daughter—the daughter I can trust. And is so you does give it back, me trust."

Ruby looked inside herself for guilt, found none. All she found was the warmth of love—and fear. "Midnight"—he kept on—"you sister call me at midnight!" Ruby's eyes went to Phyllisia, and seeing the look, he demanded, "And what she must do? We think you must fall in a crack in the sidewalk; that you fall under a train, that you knock in the head by a thief. I tell you is *midnight* she call." Now his anger included Phyllisia, who sat chastened more by her betrayal of her sister than her father's anger. And it was only then that Ruby noticed the signs of worry and sleeplessness on her sister's drawn face.

"Now tell me"—his tone changed from anger to grievance—"what about this Duprey woman?"

And there it was. Danger to her new life, to everything she wanted. And for an unknown reason, the image of Daphne as a child, walking beside her tall, black father as he held his head loftily, unaware that the sidesteps of his daughter as she skirted the newspapers were caution and not another game of potsie.

"The woman call me the other day. She sweet-talk me. She ain't yet give me she address. The telephone number she give, it ain't she house. It where she work. But what it is—some secret? Even your sister ain't know where you go?"

He looked from one to the other, baffled.

"Look at me hands." He held his hands out. They were shaking with anger, yet he went on calmly. "I ain't touch you. I ain't touching you. But if you ain't give me this woman's address and she telephone number I ain't saying what I going to do—to the two a you."

Ruby gave him the number, not because of his threat, but what was the use of lying?

"Now, what she daughter's name?"

"Daphne."

"Talk. I ain't hear good."

"Daphne."

"Daphne what?"

"Duprey."

"Oho, so is such a one as Duprey? Where she live?" There was nothing else but to tell him.

He went into the dining room and she heard him dial, heard him say, "This is Calvin Cathy. I want to talk to who in charge."

What if it was Daphne on the other end? What if she coolly told him who was really in charge? "Oho, so madam, we talk again. You see, me daughter spend the night out . . . Oho, so is there she sleep? But Madame Duprey, are you in the habit . . . Oho . . . But I give you me number . . . oho . . . and about that bogus number . . . oho . . . oho . . . oho . . ."

One hundred per they were, Mrs. Duprey and Daphne. And from Calvin's changing mood it seemed she had the capacity to gentle him. "Uhuh . . . uhuh . . . the next time it ain't for you to worry, is for me. If it get so late just put her in a cab. Uhuh . . . uhuh . . . True . . . But I ain't want me daughter to sleep outside she house . . . not again . . . uhuh . . . uhuh . . ."

He became calmer, but was still skeptical. He stared at Ruby after hanging up the phone. "Doubletalk, doubletalk. People think that everybody what come from a little island is jackass. They ain't know that doubletalk is part of a we creation.

"Look, bring this Daphne Duprey in this house to meet me. You got time to sleep at she, you got time to bring she. And that ain't doubletalk."

Considering both of their personalities, a meeting between Daphne and Calvin was bound to be dramatic, but nothing in Ruby's experience had prepeared her for their confrontation.

The day she brought Daphne home, Calvin was waiting. He was dressed in a brown tweed suit that matched his eyes, a yellow shirt that softened the sterness of his face. In her eyes he was stunningly handsome, and Ruby felt a surge of pride as she introduced him. "Daphne, this is my father."

They looked at each other and then they stared, and somehow her introduction remained unfinished and she became an onlooker. They sized up each other—perhaps admiringly. Daphne was six feet tall, Calvin, six-one. They were both elegant in stature, their clothes a part of their dominating presence as was their arrogance. One might envy, hate, even despise them, but one had to react. And they were reacting to each other in a way that was impossible to determine.

Their appraisal of each other was so long that Phyllisia, curled up on the couch ready to go back to her reading, suddenly sat up. And Ruby, having felt such great pride in Calvin, now turned to Daphne to see her out of his eyes:

She is so lovely, with those gray eyes . . . black-fringed, gray eyes . . . the crisp curl of her hair . . . the full, full mouth . . . that long unmarred flow of neck . . . her clothes so right . . . so very right . . . that silk shirt . . . concealing her breasts . . . her elegance . . . her elegance . . .

Suddenly aware of the acute silence, Calvin looked back, saw Phyllisia's inquisitive stare. He looked at Ruby, did a double take at the expression on her face, stared into her eyes summing up reasons for her fear, her intensity,

before she could again close them to him. He turned back
to Daphne, placed his hands in his back pockets, swayed
back and forth. The change in his attitude broke a spell,
and Daphne looked him up and down with the eyes she
used on big, black, handsome men.

"Oho." Calvin pulled himself together with an effort.
"So is you me daughter spend the night with?" His tone
came out harshly and triggered Daphne's charm.

"Mr. Cathy, I am so glad to meet you. I do hope that the
evening Ruby spent with me did nothing to hurt our
future relations. As Mumsy told you, it—"

"Uhuh, your Mother told me. It was late. And I told her
let we hope it ain't happen again."

"That doesn't prevent us from shaking hands, does it,
Mr. Cathy?"

Calvin had been already unnerved by his initial impression of Daphne. Her coolness unnerved him even more.
Ruby realized that Daphne's intentionally intellectual
manner put him at a disadvantage, angered him. His
hands fumbled out of his back pockets, went to meet
Daphne's—and her firm handshake appeared to anger
him still more. Roughly, he pumped her hand up and
down, up and down, trying to shake her poise. But
Daphne kept her grip firm. "Hey girl." Calvin smiled,
thinly suggestive. "But you got yourself a grip there." He
felt her biceps. "I bet you could box me head good if you
take me on."

His familiarity obviously annoyed Daphne, forced her
to take a more poised, sophisticated stance. "Take you
on? I don't understand, Mr. Cathy. One of my most highly
prized attributes is my reluctance, or, rather, my inabil-
ity, to discuss the improbable."

"True? You ain't think is possible?"

"Highly improbable, Mr. Cathy. I don't know if Ruby
has ever told you, but I pride myself in always being cool,
calm, collected, cultured, poised, refined and"—she gave
one of her toothy, charming smiles—"intelligent."

"How old you say you are?"

"I didn't. I never do. I have never believed that age is a
prerequisite for intelligence. But if it does make a differ-

ence, then the edge is on me. I don't think I'm being too presumptuous in saying that I am much younger than you."

What is happening. What is happening? Why don't they care what they are doing to me? They must know . . . they are hurting . . . hurting . . .

Calvin looked at his watch. "What time did you say you was leaving?"

"You are quite correct in anticipating me, Mr. Cathy. This is a lovely apartment. The people in it are so . . . handsome. But never fear, I shall be leaving shortly."

At least he showed some grace. He left. But in leaving he left no unanswered questions. Daphne was not welcome in this house. He did not want to see her again. And Daphne understood.

"There goes the great love of my life—out of that door," she sighed mockingly. "It was never meant to be, Bronzie, you inherited your father's good looks, but I am grateful you did not inherit his vulgarity. Vulgarity is such a bore." Her smile was tight, controlled, her anger near the surface as she turned to Phyllisia. "And you are Phyllisia? Quite a girl, I hear. What are you reading?" She glanced at the book in Phyllisia's hand.

"Agatha Christie."

"Murder mysteries." Her controlled anger made the tone one of disparagement, to which Phyllisia responded flippantly.

"Oh, I read other books too. Frantz Fanon, Chairman Mao, DuBois, Malcolm X. But every once in a while I rest my mind with trivia."

"My God, Ruby!" Daphne's anger surfaced. "Are you sure you are a member of this family? What a devastating experience!"

She walked out of the room and out of the house. "Weee," Phyllisia whistled. "That was a meeting if there ever was one. My God, Ruby. What was it all about?"

"I wish I knew," Ruby answered miserably. "I only wish I knew."

9

The gulf that separated Daphne and Calvin was deep, wide—unbridgeable, Ruby was certain. He was opposed to their friendship—that she knew too. He wanted to prevent them from meeting, but how could he? He could not stop their paths from crossing at school.

The Saturday after he met Daphne he revealed his first clumsy plan. "Look." He apologized when he came into their bedroom to discuss the week's shopping. "I ain't bring change home with me last night. After you finish your work in the house, come by the place for money to go to the show."

"What about the shopping?"

"Shopping?" He asked as though it were a new idea. "Oh, oh, you ain't mind that for today. I got this woman, Miss Effie, she say she'll look after that for we—from now on."

"From now on!"

"Yes, she . . ."

"Miss Effie? Who is she?" Phyllisia sat bolt upright.

"All you know she."

Ruby didn't, but she did not want to ask him.

"I don't . . ." Phyllisia started, but stopped when Ruby

kicked her under the covers. After Calvin left, Phyllisia turned on Ruby. "Why must I go to the movies because he decided? He didn't even ask us."

"You don't really want to stay home?"

"There is exactly where I want to stay," Phyllisia said determinedly. "I have my letter to write today."

"Write Edith when you get back."

"No, I'm writing . . ."

"Please, Phyllisia. Can't you see? He knows I will sneak out if I stay home. He wants us where he thinks he can check up on us."

"What are you saying Ruby, is that you have no courage to . . ."

"He's trying to do to me and Daphne just what he did to you and Edith."

At that, Phyllisia grew silently thoughtful, and Ruby knew she had scored. Phyllisia had never forgiven herself for her lack of courage in standing up to Calvin when he insulted her orphaned friend, Edith, forcing her to leave their house. She had even blamed him—despite his innocence in that particular act—for helping to send her friend away to an orphanage. Now they both suffered Phyllisia's imposed penance: her complete fidelity to Edith and lack of interest in other friends, even though Calvin had never admitted his wrongdoing.

"Well, all right." Phyllisia gave in. "But just this once."

When they arrived at Calvin's small, overcrowded restaurant on Seventh Avenue, it was twelve o'clock. Calvin, as usual, was busy, cooking short orders, shouting to his cook, serving crowds five deep at the counter, and relentlessly driving his counterman, who worked alongside, to match his tireless energy. It never ceased to amaze Ruby how this haggard, sweaty man always managed to emerge in seconds as the proud, faultlessly groomed, handsome Calvin Cathy who stepped out in the streets.

When he saw the girls he reached under the counter and brought out a neighborhood movie guide with theaters underlined in red. "Which one of these you want to see?" He pointed out a few on the same street. At random, Ruby chose one and Phyllisia agreed. This was a mistake. Phyllisia's objection was the barometer by which he usually gauged their compliance. Suspicion flared in his eyes.

On the way to the movie, Phyllisia complained, "That man is crazy. He don't believe you if you do and he don't believe you if you don't. You should have said you were staying home."

"It's better this way," Ruby said decisively. "Why aggravate him? It isn't too much to ask of you, is it?" Behind her words were the years of selfless services rendered. Phyllisia grumbled in response. Ruby went on. "The first picture starts at one. The second starts at . . ."

"Double features never end," Phyllisia noted dourly. "You be back here at four!"

"Okay. Wait for me in the lobby . . ."

"On second thought, you had better go in," Phyllisia broke in, grinning impishly. "If I'm not mistaken that's Daddy's car parked across the street."

The big black Buick was double-parked. A blind person could not miss it. "If that's not like the ostrich the teachers talk about," Phyllisia said gleefully. "He's looking the other way, so he thinks we can't see him."

"He knows what he's doing," Ruby answered. Undoubtedly he had parked in order to be seen, to force them to obey. They went in.

But after sitting a few minutes Ruby went to the door, where, peering out, she saw the front of his car. She kept sitting and getting up. After a few times, the usher standing near the door winked at her.

"What's happening, baby? I still got a few hours on duty but if you wait around . . ."

"It's my father," Ruby explained hastily. Why would he think she was flirting? "He's in that Buick out there, spying on me."

Immediately the usher's flirtatious manner changed. His tone became solicitous, suggesting that part of his duty was to help young ladies outwit fathers, lovers, and husbands. "Come this way."

He took her to an exit at the front of the theater, leading through an alleyway to a big iron door which opened into the next street. "Waiting out front, go out the back, dig?" He smiled broadly. "The name is Georgie. When you get back just ask for Georgie. And knock like this. Nothing to it."

Ruby looked at the thick iron door. She tried the signal. It sounded faint, hopelessly inadequate. "Are you sure you will hear?"

"You got a key or something? Knock with that. I'll hear. I'll be waiting around."

Walking to the bus stop was like walking through an open field in a Western shoot-out. Never had she realized how many big Buicks drove through the streets of Harlem. On the bus she felt safe, but once back on the street she ran all the way to Daphne's, vulnerable, expecting the car to pull alongside and a big "Oho" to fill her ears.

"God, you are eighteen, Ruby." Daphne responded to her plight with unsympathetic impatience. "This is nineteen-seventy. How can you allow yourself to be manipulated like an infant."

"Daphne, I . . ."

"Let's get to work!"

It was so unfair. After all her efforts to get no sympathy, no love, no kiss, no Bronzie.

"Ruby, I have been discussing this with you for the last hour, in what I consider the most elevated manner. You have not been listening." Tense, controlled, she pushed back her chair. Ruby caught her hand.

"Daphne, I am sorry. I thought you would understand."

"Understand what, Ruby? That I am wasting my time?"

"That—about Dad?"

"If you refuse to grow up, that has to be your concern. If you allow that . . . that . . ." For the first time, Ruby saw her at a loss for words.

"Give me time, Daphne. He'll calm down. That meeting was—Daphne, don't let him come between us. I would rather die."

"Let that big, blustering egomaniac come between us?

I'll see him in hell first! But I'm not going to be put down, Ruby. I'm not going to be the one who suffers!"

"I'm suffering. I'm suffering too, Daphne." Daphne kissed her hands, sat back at the desk, and they went on with the lessons. But then it was time to go, and the tension, the smoldering eyes, the obviously controlled anger became evident.

"Bronzie, this is Saturday. Weekends are our time. It is only three-thirty."

"Phyllisia is waiting."

"Will Ruby meet Phyllisia on time?" she mocked. "Will the two little girls get to the house before the wicked monster? Ruby, this is a joke!"

But Ruby left, in fear. Daphne's philosophy seemed more important than life to her, and she was forcing her to compromise. There was no doubt that Daphne was anything but cool, calm, and collected when she left.

"Hey, baby, you make it all right?" Jovial Georgie was waiting at the door.

"Yes, thank you so much."

"Any time, baby. Any time."

"Then I'll see you next week?"

"You wanna bet?"

"God, Ruby." Phyllisia greeted her. "It's bad enough to sit through *one* of these pictures, but to repeat . . ."

"Please, Phyllisia, I can't stand any more now."

His car was outside and they walked stiff-necked, not looking. When they got home the telephone was ringing. It was Calvin. "How did you like the show?"

"It was all right."

"Good. Look Ruby, that Hernandez woman called. She picking you and your sister up tomorrow to take you to she house for dinner. She coming at twelve o'clock."

Dinner with the Hernandezes was a family affair as usual, and as usual it was elegant. Family, from infant cousins to grandparents, sat around a large, luxuriously set table, eating a variety of succulent meats, with rice and beans, salad and fruit, and drinking a variety of wines —a repast which lasted for hours. Ruby had enjoyed it before, but now it seemed a waste of time, the people a burden, rather than the warm, sincere people she had loved.

"I am so glad you could come, Ruby." Consuela expressed her gratitude. "It seems to me we have not been so friendly since that terrible teacher makes me help her."

"No Consuela, it isn't that. I have to study. My marks have been so bad—and the term is almost over."

"My Consuela is not so smart in school." Mrs. Hernandez, a shapely, vivacious woman, leaned toward Ruby. "But what does it matter? For a girl it is not important. She will be getting married soon."

"Consuela?"

"Yes. She is already nineteen. She cannot go to school forever."

"What are your plans?" Mr. Hernandez leveled soft, sensuous eyes at Ruby, and she blushed.

"My father wants me to go to college."

"College? That is no place for beautiful girls."

"It is my father's wish." Ruby looked at Consuela and was struck anew by her placid, passionless face. "Who is he? The boy you will marry?"

"Boy?" Mr. Hernandez laughed softly. "I would not trust my daughter in the keeping of a boy."

"His name is Frederique Garcia. He is a friend of my father's," Consuela said. "He is a very wealthy man."

"And your father," Mrs. Hernandez insisted, "has he chosen no one for you?"

"No, he would not choose my husband."

She was thankful there was this difference in their islands. But if Calvin did choose, what kind of man would it be? She smiled to herself. The man Calvin would choose had not yet been born.

The week that followed was unusually hard for Ruby. She began to feel strains developing in her relationship with Daphne. To hide it they worked hard, scarcely speaking. When Ruby left, Daphne kissed her lightly. "Sorry I can't go to the bus Bronzie, but I must finish up here." It seemed Daphne was glad to be rid of her. But Ruby knew it was her way of forcing her to take a stand.

I will . . . I will take a stand . . . as soon as I am secure . . . secure. I will talk to him . . . I will tell him that I am of age . . . that I shall go where I choose . . . do what I will.

That Saturday again Calvin gave the faceless Effie their shopping chores and designated the time and place they should be—another movie on the same block. Phyllisia fumed. "Ruby, I am not going to give up my weekends to trail around with you. I have things to do, letters to write. Why don't you just tell your father that you cannot be pushed around?"

They went so far as to tell him they would not go to the movie of his choice. They wanted to go to the same theater as last week. "The same movie?" he asked, not believing them.

"It's a different picture, Daddy." Phyllisia reassured him. "That's what counts." Still grumbling and suffering from her need for her couch and book, she told Ruby, "If he can't think up better ideas than this, I refuse to come down to his level of thinking. This is the *last* Saturday."

Daphne did not make a scene. "If that old-fashioned fart likes to be deceived, so be it." But they had lost—were losing—their closeness. They worked more, touched less, were less affectionate, unable to relax. And when they finally felt more relaxed it was time to go. "What about tomorrow?" Daphne asked this at the door. "Dinner again at the Hernandezes?"

"No, that's impossible. They didn't invite us and they probably won't—not so soon. I'll be here, Daphne, early." Then, seeing the skepticism in her eyes, she said, "I swear I'll be here."

"Just in case." Daphne shrugged, kissed her, held her close. "Just in case," she repeated. "Let that do until Monday."

Ruby was late getting back to the theater, and when she signaled there was no response. She tried the door, but it was locked. Georgie had probably gone to another part of the theater. She waited a few minutes before knocking again. There was still no answer. She called, "Georgie, Georgie," realizing the futility. Her voice could not penetrate that iron door. She waited and knocked with her key, then decided to try and make it through the front.

Hugging the buildings as she turned the corner into the next street, she darted in and out of stores, keeping her head turned not to see him and so to deny that he could have seen her. In this way she finally came to the theater, darted in and up to the ticket-taker. "Is Georgie here?"

"Georgie? Naw. He left about a half hour ago."

"He usually lets me in—I mean I was already in—but I —my sister is in there."

"Where's the stub?"

"Stub?" She stared stupidly for a moment, not understanding.

"Yeah, stub, stub. You know, ticket stub." He was a squat man with an unbelieving face.

She searched her pockets, her bag, then remembered that Phyllisia had handed in the tickets. "My sister has them."

"No jive?" He sneered, not believing her.

"Look, I don't want to see the movie. All I want is my sister."

"Not without the stub!" The face bunched with determination.

"Why do you have to be so nasty?"

"Because I don't like wise chicks. If you had asked to go in, okay. But don't try to pull . . ."

"Look, my sister is . . ."

"Outta the way. People's behind you." He brushed her aside to collect tickets from the people who had lined up behind her. She stepped in front of a door that opened suddenly, looked in, saw the curtain, heard the voices from the screen, and slipped in.

"Hey you!" Ruby ran to the far side—the opposite side from where Phyllisia was sitting. Rushing down to the center of the theater, she tried to cross to the next aisle, but a comfortably settled fat woman, looking down the row of seats, said, "I don't know where you're going honey, but there ain't no seats in here."

Ruby would have tried the next row, but looking back, she saw an usher walking toward her, flashlight blinking. She crouched, hurried to the front of the theater, and started for the next aisle.

"Get outta the way." "What you think, you're a piece a glass?" "Sure can't see through her!" A chorus of voices. She crouched lower, scurried to reach the next aisle.

"She's up front. I seen her."

The voice came from the back of the theater. Ruby panicked. She ran into another winking flashlight. Frantically she worked her way through a row of knees, circled again to the front, ran across to the last section, where on hands and knees she began to count the rows. "One . . . two . . . three." Phyllisia was near the center. How could she tell the center? "Seven . . . eight . . . nine"

"Lost something, baby? Get the usher."

"No, no, it's okay."

"Let me . . ."

"Thank you, no." She scrambled away. "Ten . . . Phyllisia," she whispered.

"Got her!" Flashlights approached from both directions. Ruby stood up, shouted "Phyllisia!"

"Will you shut up?"

"Grab her!"

"Ruby?" A figure stood up in a center row.

"For God's sake what's happening in the goddamn place?"

"Phyllisia! Here."

Two men closed in from both sides; they grabbed Ruby and hustled her up the aisle.

"What are you doing! Get your hands off my sister!" Phyllisia galloped up the aisle, jumped on the back of one of the ushers, grabbed him around the neck and held on.

Letting go of Ruby, he grabbed Phyllisia, forcing her head back by her hair. She bit his hand, and he gave her a push that landed her on her back.

"What the hell you doing to that girl?" A man called

from his seat. Another voice chimed in, "I seen him. He hit her. What he think? He owns the show?"

Anxious to avoid a scene, the usher picked Phyllisia up like a bag of potatoes, flung her over his shoulder, and he and the other usher, who was hustling Ruby up the aisle, opened the door, shoved them through the lobby into the street, where they landed on their backsides.

Scrambling to her feet, Phyllisia ran back toward the closed door, shouting, "Mother ass! You damn mother ass!" Ruby looked around for the black Buick. It was not there. She dragged Phyllisia away, struggling and shouting at the theater. "Just watch, you mother ass, watch and see if I ever come to your blasted movie again!"

10

With an audacity unique to her, Ruby went out Sunday morning before Calvin awakened. It was a perfect morning. Her daring, the weather, and finding when she got to Daphne's that Mrs. Duprey had spent the night out made it the most perfect of mornings.

"Bronzie," Daphne praised her, "you have taken a most important step toward freedom." And she had. She had turned off fear and anxiety, all thoughts of home and Calvin, as she would a faucet. The day was free, free from the hovering expectations, the intrusions of adults.

Ruby and Daphne, lying in bed, had no desire to mar the day with study. They played like children. On her way to the bathroom, Ruby noticed the closet in Mrs. Duprey's room and decided to hide in it. After a long time, Daphne began looking. She searched every room before finally opening the closet door. Ruby dashed out, screaming with laughter, and the rest of the morning was spent playing childhood games—hide-and-seek, tag, even patty-cake.

At lunchtime Daphne made triple-decker hamburgers with onions and tomatoes on toasted English muffins, too large to fit into their mouths. This too was a cause for side-splitting laughter.

"Bronzie, why don't you come and stay here? Leave that miserable father and smart-assed sister of yours to each other."

"Pray tell." Ruby laughed, using one of Daphne's pet terms. "And what will Madame Duprey say? I can just see your Mumsy flipping out when I move in."

"Mumsy wouldn't mind . . . and if she did?" Daphne shrugged.

"Are you serious?"

"Of course. I don't say things I don't mean."

"But Daphne, how can you expect your mother to take care of me?"

"She'll manage. She always does." Daphne's offhand manner sobered Ruby.

"I wouldn't accept it."

"Why not? It isn't as though it will be for long. You will be graduated soon."

"I have four years in college."

"College! Bronzie, you're not really thinking of going to college?"

"Yes. My father . . ."

"Your father is an old-fashioned, West Indian blow-top —the typical primitive who thinks that making it from a small island automatically qualifies their children for world rule. You should be thinking of getting a job—going into nurses' training."

"Daphne, I don't—"

"Bronzie, you are just not college material."

"And you are?"

"Do you doubt it?"

Ruby stared across the kitchen table at Daphne and it occurred to her that this tall, well-built girl was capable of extreme coldness, of cruelty, and had a remarkable ability in justifying it.

"What if *you* don't make it into college?"

"Well fathers! How ever did you come up with such a thought? I *am* going to college, Bronzie. And not only that—one of the best. I must have told you I applied to

Brandeis. I took the test. I am sure I passed. If brains are the criterion, I am already in. If not, Mumsy and I have ways."

"Anyway, your mother has a burden enough with *your* big plans. She certainly doesn't need me to add to them."

Her petulance softened Daphne. "Bronzie, love, I hurt you. I'm sorry." She reached out to cup Ruby's face in her hands. At that moment the telephone rang. They froze. It rang and rang. By the time it stopped, so had the perfection of the day. "That certainly wasn't Mumsy. She would never ring more than four times."

It was late afternoon when they set about restoring the house to order. "I guess we should do some studying," Daphne suggested.

"I don't feel like it," Ruby answered. Daphne appeared not to notice the subtle change that her words had brought about. It was silly to be hurt, to be still chafing from her thoughtless remarks. Daphne had said she was sorry—but she hadn't taken anything back, she had not changed her mind.

"Yes, I know." Daphne stretched, yawned, scratched her stomach through her see-through pajamas. "It has been a relaxing day—too relaxing. Let's go out in the sun, visit a museum, walk up to Mumsy's."

"But we can't go out!" The faucet for her anxieties had been turned on by the ringing telephone, and suddenly Harlem and the great outdoors seemed a threat. Every street, every avenue led directly to Calvin. In the house, the telephone had rung and had not been answered. Now the doorbell might ring, and the door not be opened. But outside the seven-league Buick was just a hair's-breadth away.

"As I live and breathe! What are we, prisoners?" Daphne's eyes darkened in anger. "Ruby Cathy, your step toward freedom was certainly limited. You must stop this nonsense! You are not a child. You must tell your father!"

"You don't understand, Daphne."

"What don't I understand? That you haven't got the guts to go out in this ugly world?"

And what about her? What made her so privileged? All
she had was a mother. "We are really a very close family,
Daphne."

Daphne stiffened. Her eyes narrowed. "Do tell! And
who am I to intrude? Pray, why deceive him on my account? And why, above all things, expect me to imprison
myself on his behalf?"

They left the house together, Daphne going her way
and Ruby going hers.

The coolness of the previous week was nothing to compare to the near freeze of the week that followed.
Daphne, blatantly showing a preference to be alone,
strode off after school and Ruby had to trot to keep up
with her. She fought to get on the same subway car, then
trailed home after her like a puppy.

Daphne ignored her and always, when they reached
the door, looked as though she weighed the possibility of
refusing her entry. She never did.

The evenings were spent working, with no letup. With
a singleness of purpose, Daphne pulled out countless papers, book after book, submerging herself in her work
with such concentration that Ruby felt shut out completely. Guilt-ridden, Ruby endured the humiliation, the
indifference, trying to match her friend's single-minded
absorption in her own work. As long as she sat there, as
long as she did her best to keep up, Daphne allowed her
space. But by Wednesday of that week, the silence had
punctured her concentration. She reached over to grab
Daphne's hands: "Please, let's talk. I know I was wrong."

"Well fathers!" Daphne interrupted her in astonishment. "Ruby, you are the most selfish—I spend so much
time helping you with your lessons that you seem to forget that I must study too. What do we have to talk about
that we haven't discussed already? The finals are on us.
We have to study, study."

Was she selfish? Daphne spoke the truth. She had been
helping Ruby, neglecting her own work. Yet she seemed
to want to. Ruby tried to force herself to concentrate,

frightened at the thought that if she lagged Daphne would close the door on her.

Saturday Calvin interrupted a week-long silence. "Look." He woke them up, apologizing. "I feel bad—bad. I ain't spend enough time with you daughters." Ruby and Phyllisia tensed. He had pretended nothing had happened but Ruby knew that whatever was coming was caused by her last Sunday's absence. It had to be bad news. "I always plan to spend time but something always happen." Apologies sounded unnatural from him. "This time I put me foot down. If other folk can do it, I can do it. From now on, Sunday is family day in this house, I spending it with you. Effie coming to cook tomorrow. Today she start fixing. I inviting some people."

"That," Phyllisia said when Calvin closed the door, "is a gentleman." And, as his footsteps faded, she added, "And a goddamn hypocrite. And that woman, whoever she is, joins the Great Cathy on my watchamacallit list. Sight unseen, I hate her!"

The sinking feeling in her stomach forced Ruby to lie still. What did Phyllisia's words matter? What did Calvin's new tactics matter? Except he was clever. If she disobeyed him today it could mean the final split with Daphne.

"What I think we should do, Ruby, is to refuse to let this 'Effie' in."

"How can you hate her? You don't even know her!"

"That is one thing I got from my father," Phyllisia said smugly. "I can hate *her* in the same way *he* can hate girls young enough to be his daughters—for no reason at all, except to make our lives a misery. And if she messes with me, I'm going to make her the most miserable woman who ever lived on this earth."

Ruby was crushed when she called Daphne. "I didn't expect you anyway." Daphne's voice was cold, distant. "I know your father's primitive mind. His next step had to be the ball and chain. I don't know anyone who deserves it more than you."

11

Miss Effie turned out to be a woman they had seen once before—at their mother's funeral. Tall, broad, matronly, regal, she stalked into the apartment, reviving memories. "You poor dears," she exclaimed. "Words cannot express how I grieved for you poor, motherless children. My, but you did grow. I would hardly know you now, but thanks to Calvin . . ."

She left them at the door, gaping, as she marched down the hall. She stopped to put her things in the hall closet and went straight to the kitchen like a homing pigeon.

"I tell you, I can't stand her," Phyllisia hissed. "I remember at Mother's funeral, she talked about Mother having so much class and stuff, and how it was too bad she couldn't take it with her."

"So, what does it matter now?"

"It matters. Who does she think she is, coming in here and taking over? And as for class, she looks like she's been working at it all her life. Somebody must have forced her to say prunes, stew, poo, since the day she was born."

Ruby laughed, thinking of the full-lipped children on the Island, forced to repeat words like stew and prunes to control their thick lips. In Miss Effie's case, it had worked.

Her full lips were properly prim—even though her eyes
were as rapacious as those of a vulture.

Their "company" turned out to be Mr. Charles and
Cousin Frank, who visited them so regularly they were
almost like family, and Calvin's "day" turned out to be
the two hours he took off to eat.

"Oh Ruby"—Phyllisia joked at Calvin's scheming—
"we having a fete. People coming. Mr. Charles, Cousin
Frank, and Calvin. Let's get out the steel band."

Despite the other flaws she found in Miss Effie, Phyllisia
found none in her cooking. More than that, Miss Effie had
prepared some of their favorite dishes from the Island:
Creole chicken, roast pork, stewed red beans, stewed
eggplant, white rice, avocados, yams, plantains, and let-
tuce salad. A feast! Shelving her hatred, Phyllisia ate so
much that her gluttony was embarrassing. So did Calvin.

Miss Effie hovered, anxious to please him. "Dear, is
there something more I can get you?" Or, "Is it the way
you like, Calvin dear?" After a time Ruby realized that
her father's attention was riveted to his plate, compli-
menting Effie by his appetite while hiding his lack of
interest in her as a woman. Ruby began to pity the over-
anxious cook.

"What happened to those pretty brown eyes?" Mr.
Charles, noticing Ruby's silence, touched her arm. "It
seem to me they looking sad."

"Nothing." She managed to smile.

"How you mean what happen?" Cousin Frank raised
his head to wink at her. "Is spring. The girl in love. Any
fool can see that." Calvin stuffed his mouth as though he
were starving, and Miss Effie took time out from him to
voice concern for Ruby.

"But you are not eating, dear. Are you ill?"

"I don't eat much," Ruby apologized. Calvin glared at
her. But before he could say anything, Miss Effie took up
the serving dish.

"Let me bring some more stewed chicken, Calvin
dear."

"No, no. Is enough, enough."

"Come now, Calvin—a big man like you. You must keep up your strength." Phyllisia choked on a sip of water, and all three men smiled into their plates to keep from looking at Phyllisia. Ruby looked from Calvin to Phyllisia.

Are we that close . . . I don't feel close . . . look at him . . . at Phyllisia . . . eating like pigs . . . they don't care about me . . . they don't even know that I am dying of unhappiness . . . they can't even see . . . eat . . . eat . . . eat . . . pigs . . . hogs . . . Daphne, Daphne. . . . will you eat out with Mumsy? You will be charming, sarcastic . . . and she will hit back . . . angry . . . flippant . . . approving . . . you are close . . . closer than we here . . . why did I say we were close . . . close?

"Yes man, the world does change." Mr. Charles, finished eating, reared back in his chair. "Thank God it happen in my time." He reached for a toothpick. "I remember when they did say the sun ain't set one minute on British soil. Is so they tell us in school. Now man, the sun give Britain one wink and it gone. This is the power now."

Calvin looked up from his plate to say, "How come you think I here in America?"

"You slip through on a quota," Frank joked.

"No man, is because the eagle that spread over the world originate here," Calvin parried. "And I like originality. This is the greatest power of all time."

"But ain't any power of its time the greatest power of all time. Remember when Britannia ruled the waves?"

"Is a question a degree."

"Is a question a change. The one constant is change," Frank said dogmatically.

"Change is everything," the soft-spoken Charles interjected. "Weapons change. The question has always been who got the weapons to kill the most people."

"So!" Calvin bellowed. "What to stop this country from ruling the world?"

"Black Power," Phyllisia chimed in.

"Ch—upps." Calvin sucked his back teeth disparagingly. "Don't talk stupidness."

"Let the children talk nuh, man," Frank protested. "The time gone when women and children stop in the background."

"Oh God, don't tell Calvin that." Charles laughed. "You want the man to dead? If time go any place it go around him. That is a man who ain't want nothing to change."

"Go on girl," Cousin Frank encouraged. Phyllisia went on proudly to display her new nationalism. "The United States is made up of black people and white people, right?"

"Well, it got some others"—Cousin Frank tempered—"but go on."

"And the white people started this thing called prejudice, right?"

"Well, they ain't exactly start it. It been around. But go on."

"They froze it though," Phyllisia insisted. "Americans go all over the world calling people niggers and japs and gooks, and spades and chinky eyes, and—all kinds of things."

"True—go on."

"And the world is made up of black people, so . . ."

"How you mean, black people?" Calvin exploded in annoyance. "Korea, they black? Vietnam, they black? China, they . . ."

"The Third World, Daddy. The Third World as a force. That's Black Power."

"She ain't doing bad a-tall." Frank toasted Phyllisia with a glass of water. "Ride on little lady."

"That's encouraging her in stupidness." Calvin raised his voice to drown out the others. "Is money power that count. It count yesterday. It count today. And it count tomorrow."

"And what have you to say on the subject?" Mr. Charles smiled at Ruby invitingly. Ruby blinked. She had only been half listening.

"I—I suppose there is truth in both viewpoints. The, ah, the Third World force, as Phyllisia says, has been colonized for so long. With their development, their natural resources and all of that, well, uhm, they will be a force to reckon with one day. Money is only important in what it can buy . . ." She broke off, confused, and silence greeted her statement. They had never heard her express herself—indeed, politics had never been a part of her thinking—and it came as a surprise, even to her, that she had been able to gather these diverse thoughts. Looking into their interested faces, she felt hers suddenly flame in embarrassment and she stammered, could not go on.

In the middle of their silence the telephone rang. Ruby jumped up. So did Calvin. "I'll take that," he said sharply. Ruby sat. Everyone looked into his plate, waiting. "Hello . . . hello . . . I say hello . . ." He came back to his seat, darting a suspicious glance at Ruby. Cousin Frank searched his pockets for a cigar, lit it, puffed a while, then, smiling expansively, said: "Well Miss Ruby. You are full of surprises. That was quite a talk you did make. It is good to see that you are not only beautiful but intelligent. That is a rare . . ."

"But it was always so," Charles interrupted, "She was always thoughtful too. And now she is getting to the age— Tell me Ruby, a birthday must be coming up. How old will you be?"

"Nineteen," Ruby whispered, not trusting her voice. *Who had been calling? Who would call and not answer?*

"Nineteen," Frank cried. "A young lady here. Time for making plans for the future."

Everyone had finished eating, but Calvin suddenly re-filled his plate and dug in again. "Yes"—Frank examined the end of his cigar—"we old folks won't always be around, and one must always have a plan."

"Old?" Calvin scoffed. "Who old around here?"

"Nineteen, huh?" Charles said dreamily, ignoring Calvin. "Oh God, Frank! To be nineteen again! *That* was the time of romance and beauty."

Calvin kept stuffing himself and the two other men let the silence deepen. Then Mr. Charles perked up. "What happen to that boy . . . you know, the one Calvin gave a bloody nose?"

"But I agree with dear Calvin." Miss Effie felt sufficiently informed to butt in. "He did the right thing. If a child is to finish school . . ."

"How you agreeing?" Calvin got to his feet, pushed back his chair. "How you agreeing, and I ain't say nothing?"

Miss Effie did not leave with Calvin and the guests, and this seemed a part of Calvin's program. She pulled up a chair in front of the television set just as Phyllisia had curled up to read behind her on the couch. "Dearie, put down that book and come watch this show. It's my favorite. I never miss it."

"Then why don't you go home and watch it?"

Miss Effie took the broad hint with grace. She didn't budge. Ruby, uninterested in the program, was sitting in a stuffed chair. Phyllisia finally put down her book, stared at Miss Effie, and assumed a fake interest in the program.

"Who is that?" she asked innocently.

"That's Marcus Welby, M.D."

"No he's not—he's a blasted phoney," Phyllisia taunted. "He's the father on *Father Knows Best.*"

"He used to be, but now he's Doctor . . ."

"What do you mean, used to be? If he used to be he still is. You mean he just abandoned all of his children to go and pose as a doctor?"

"You must understand," Miss Effie began. But the rest of her sentence was drowned out by Phyllisia's loud protest.

"Ruby, suppose our father all of a sudden decided that he was no longer Calvin Cathy, owner of the greasy spoon, and called himself Doctor Jones or Doctor Johnson. What would you say to that?"

Ruby shook her head, knowing it was useless to sidetrack Phyllisia. "Can you imagine that?"

"Sshh," Miss Effie said, "I can't hear . . ."

"Taking knives and sticking them into people instead

of roast beef." The irrepressible Phyllisia continued, shouting, "Murder! That's what it would be, murder!" She rushed in front of the television set, blocking Miss Effie's view, shouting, "Murderer! Murderer!"

12

Miss Effie came every weekend—Saturday to shop and Sunday to prepare the food. Calvin came home Sundays to eat, and Ruby often wondered if he paid her.

How could she tolerate Phyllisia's rudeness if she wasn't being paid? Ruby wondered. Phyllisia did not let the poor woman rest. All week she planned a list of petty annoyances to plague Miss Effie. Nothing seemed to penetrate her thick skin, her dull mentality except the pleasure she derived from Calvin's big appetite. Phyllisia persisted. "If we leave her alone she might make the mistake of thinking that she is welcome," the girl grumbled, "and she might try to move in!"

Ruby pitied the woman. In a way she felt a sort of kinship because of the way Daphne treated her. Just as Calvin let Miss Effie come to serve his needs—doubtful as those needs seemed to the girls—so Daphne let Ruby visit to fulfill something. Ruby supposed that Miss Effie must be telling herself the same thing Ruby repeated to herself a dozen times a day. "I would not be here if she didn't want me. She would not let me come if she did not care." Even Daphne's half-hearted invitation did not put her at ease. "You are welcome to stay if you are here to work,

Ruby. But I must tell you that I don't have much
time . . ."

"You are letting him break us up, Daphne."

"No. You are."

"He's my father, and . . ."

"Look, Ruby, if you are not here to work I will have to
ask you to leave." And Ruby worked on in silence.

Like Miss Effie, Ruby had to be grateful for small favors.
Daphne allowed her to sit near her while they worked.
She worked diligently, silently, getting up only after she
was finished to kiss Daphne on the forehead, letting her
breasts brush Daphne's arm. And she left happier, knowing she still had this power. For the time it was enough.
She could wait. Things would be like before.

Then one morning Miss Gottlieb came in with Miss
Schwartz, another teacher. Consuela was absent, and
Miss Schwartz had come to help Miss Gottlieb with the
chores Consuela and Ruby had done previously. Before
leaving, Miss Schwartz leaned over the desk to whisper to
Miss Gottlieb, who looked up, snarling at the class. "Who?
Them? Who can get that bunch to do anything? They are
a lousy bunch. I can barely wait until they leave my room,
with their smell of eyetalian garlic and nigger sweat."

Miss Schwartz quickly withdrew, flashing a look of apol-
ogy around the room, head down, her face red. "Did you
hear that?" Georgio said to Ruby as they went to the next
class. "Tell that to your friend Consuela and see whether
she still wants to help that ugly old hag."

"I certainly shall," answered Ruby. She was glad to
have been freed from the thanklessness of helping Miss
Gottlieb. Never, never again would she allow herself to
be used in such a way by anyone so evil. She went from
class to class, feeling elated. Not only was she free of her
sympathy for the cripple, but she was going to free herself from all Calvin's schemes, the Miss Effie weekends,
movies, the lot. This very evening she would stay with
Daphne.

A fire drill ended the day. Instead of rushing out of
their classes, the students had to adhere to the rigid disci-

pline of the drill: forming orderly lines, marching from their classrooms behind their teachers. Class followed class out to the street.

Miss Gottlieb's room was the last one in the corridor to be vacated. Miss Gottlieb dragged herself to the closet for her coat. There was no one to help her. Miss Schwartz couldn't leave her own class, and the lined-up students had no intention of lending a hand. Grabbing at her coat, she pivoted on her good leg. The coat fell, and as she reached to catch it, so did her cane. She stood, staring helplessly down at the fallen stick. The room grew still.

"My cane, my cane," she whispered hoarsely. Without the cane she was lost. The students stared at the cane in fascination, then stared in a body at the teacher. Nothing was near enough for her to grab on to.

She looked around wildly—not at anyone, or anything, for she expected nothing, except perhaps a miracle. Slowly she bent her knees, then with a movement of her hip thrust out the crippled leg. It curled around the cane. She dragged it toward her, near, nearer. But as though by a whim of its own, the cane swirled away. She pulled herself up, stared at the cane in bewilderment. The class waited as she repeated the motion, twisting her body toward the floor. Sweat stood out on the balding head, sparkled through wispy strands of hair. Down, lower, lower, her body quivering, her balance wavering. Quickly she drew herself tall.

The room a few doors away began to empty. Footsteps resounding throughout the long corridor added a sense of suspense to the tense room. The teacher tried again, bending her knee, lowering her body in desperation. Her only choice was to allow herself to fall, to drag herself along the floor, under the hostile stares of her students, to the elusive cane.

Another room emptied. Tramp, tramp, tramp, soldiers on a long march. Tramp, tramp, tramp, the footsteps faded. Another class began to empty. Tramp, tramp, tramp, the marching steps, whispers, giggles, soft laughter slithering into the room, curling around the stillness, fading, fading, fading. The silence of an empty school engulfed them.

The twisted, tortured body went down, down. "I smell smoke!"

A malicious snicker broke the tension.

"Yeah, me too."

"We better get the hell out!"

"We'll go up in flames!"

Yet no one moved. The teacher's torment mesmerized them. Even if there had been a fire, they could not have moved. Waiting to see her perish, they would have perished with her, so tightly did she bind them with her hatred.

For Ruby, it was the most painful moment she had ever experienced, the most shameful. She tried to recall each insult, each humiliation that the cripple had forced her to endure. Still, the sight of the tortured body, the unequal struggle for a simple right, knotted her heart, suffocated her. Sweat poured from her forehead. Blood rushed to her face, burning it, blurring her vision. *Give me strength . . . give me strength . . . I shall not go to her . . . I dare not go to her . . . dear God . . . help her . . . help her . . .*

Miss Gottlieb looked at her angrily, as though demanding, How dare you pray for me? She would not beg. She did not expect prayers, she expected nothing from the smelly eyetalians, the sweaty niggers.

And Ruby suddenly did not want her to beg. She could not bear it if she begged. She stepped out of line. Georgio, anticipating her, grabbed her arm. "Don't be no fool. She can do it. Let her."

She pulled away from the restraining hand, walked to the front of the room, picked up the cane, went to the teacher, helped her to her feet, picked up the coat, shook the rag-doll arm into the sleeve with more gentleness than she had ever shown, and handed the cane to Miss Gottlieb. Head high, she returned to her place in line, not daring to look at her fellow students. She had betrayed them. She was sorry. She was relieved. She had done what she had to do. *Daphne, Daphne, Daphne . . .*

Daphne had walked quickly away when the class was dismissed. "Daphne," Ruby called, running and catching her arm. The tall girl whirled, threw off the restraining hand, stared at Ruby, her eyes dark with anger. Then she pivoted away and continued down the street. Ruby gazed after her until she'd rounded the corner.

It's over . . . it's over . . . it's over . . . dear God . . . how can I live . . . how can I breathe . . . how can I go on? It's over.

13

The giant red candle's flickering was too weak to have caused the eruptions of hot wax that flowed down its sides like lava, only to drip insistently from the altar of darkness on which it stood. Like the red lamp in Daphne's room, the glow was symbolic, but the drip, drip, dripping was real. As though to emphasize its usefulness, the candle flickered and went out, but the drip, drip, drip went on. Drip, drip, drip on the same spot.

I am going to die . . . I am going to die. Pain, fear, anxiety. Suddenly wide awake, Ruby sat up in bed, clutched her stomach, clawed at nerve ends which, like recently broken strings of a tightly wound violin, quivered, quivered, quivered. Why was she dying? She did not want to die. Fearfully she groped around the darkness, her hands contacting a warm body. Phyllisia, Phyllisia. She breathed easier, sighed, eased under the covers and curved herself around her sister's sleeping body.

But fear kept quickening the muscles of her stomach. She gave into it, moved away from her sister. *Daphne . . . Daphne . . .* Daphne had gone out of her life. She tried to sleep, even though sleep was meaningless now.

Determined to remain in bed, she nevertheless found
herself wandering to the kitchen. Four-thirty—she had
probably been awakened by her father. She opened the
refrigerator, closed it, listened at her father's door, wanting to go in. His heavy breathing reached her. What did
she have to say to him? Nothing. Absolutely nothing. She
entered the dining room, fingered the telephone. "Well
fathers, at this time of the morning?" She imagined the
mocking voice. It was a game she played, over and over
again. "Pray tell, are you going to wet my welcome mat
again? Well fathers . . ." Ruby went into the living room
and stood looking out into the dark street. It was silent,
her guardian tree a shadow adding to the darkness.

After a time she crawled back into bed, putting her
arms around Phyllisia once more. But Phyllisia was near
enough to wakefulness to resist and shrug her off. Ruby
let her arm fall away. *I do feel this emptiness . . . I am
dead . . . I will die . . . I have no one . . . I am alone
. . . Daphne is alone too.*

The bell rang. All the muscles of Ruby's body jerked
into awareness. She strained, listening. It was her imagi-
nation. The bell rang again. Ruby sprang up, ran barefoot
down the hall, heard her father still snoring, raced to the
door, her heart beating. She opened it.

"The weatherman say it's going to rain all day so I
decided to beat the rain."

Miss Effie stepped regally into the apartment and
Ruby, speechless at the dawn intrusion, finally squeaked
out, "What are you doing here? It's so early . . ."

"Nonsense, it's seven-thirty, almost eight." Miss Effie's
presence filled the apartment with the strange muskiness
of order, respectability—the unmistakable fragrance of
hope-chest sachet. "Your father still asleep?"

"Daddy doesn't get up until late on Sundays."

"Good. I'm glad I got here in time to fix his breakfast."

With that, the woman walked down the hall to the
closet and began putting away her things. Ruby went
back to her room, shaken by the violence of her desire to
strike Miss Effie with some weapon, any weapon. *I am*

going mad . . . dear God! I never wanted to injure, to murder. I am mad!

"Who was that?" Phyllisia's sleepy voice came muffled from the covers.

"Who do you think?"

Phyllisia struggled sleepily to a sitting position. "No! What does she want? At this hour?"

"She's come to fix Daddy's breakfast—I think."

"She's his fucking cook! His fucking servant!"

"What kind of language is that?" Ruby protested.

"How the fuck does she think he managed before the bib and spoon?" Phyllisia settled angrily back into the bed. After a few minutes, during which Ruby thought she had fallen asleep again, Phyllisia said thoughtfully, "I don't know about you, Ruby, but I, for one, am going to do something drastic to get that woman out—and keep her out—of this house."

"Like what?"

"Like letting a cage of mice loose under her chair."

"Ch—upps." Ruby sucked her back teeth. Sometimes Phyllisia used more energy in thinking up the impossible than the possible. One little mouse would have Phyllisia climbing walls. "Go back to sleep if you can't think up one better than that."

"I'll think of something, don't you worry," Phyllisia promised.

They lay silently, neither wanting to get up for fear of bumping into Miss Effie. "I guess I'll have my breakfast in bed," Phyllisia mused.

"If she brings breakfast in bed for anyone, it won't be *you*."

"Not Miss Effie—you."

"Me?"

"Yes, you, Ruby. What's the matter? You don't spoil me any more."

Just then they heard Miss Effie knocking on Calvin's door, heard her ask, "Calvin dear, are you awake?"

What magnificent presumption! The girls sat up with their mouths open, staring at each other. They had never dared disturb Calvin's rest. His own body-timer took care of that. And he could be an absolute monster if wakened artificially. "Calvin? Calvin, dear?"

"What happen? What time it is? It ain't day yet!"

Miss Effie murmured in response, and he growled, "No man, it can't be more than eight, eight-fifteen, thirty the most." Yes, he knew. He had an innate, primitive time sense. Without sun or clock, he knew.

"The man promise rain." Miss Effie repeated her excuse. "I thought it best to beat the rain." He was silent.

"And I fix a nice breakfast."

"What the hell you mean, waking me up at the middle of the night talking breakfast! Is sleep I want! Is sleep I need! I eat food any damn time I please!"

"But Calvin dear . . ."

"Don't 'dear' me. Get the hell outta me room. Let me sleep!"

"*That's* good to know," Phyllisia said, and smirked.

"But we know that already. Daddy never wants—"

"Not *that*, Ruby. It's good to know that he just brings her in the house to provoke *us*. I'll make him pay—and pay good. Give me time."

The day proved as dismal as Miss Effie's weatherman had predicted. Gray clouds grew grayer, hung lower, and before the morning was over a heavy drizzle had started, which turned to a heavy downpour, punctuated with thunder and lightning. The gloom of the house grew with the gloom outside.

Restlessly, Ruby walked from one room to the next, keeping out of Miss Effie's way. She wound up spending most of her time in the room where her mother had sewed, now crowded with the odds and ends she had refused to throw away. Ruby looked out the window. Unimportant details in the backyard absorbed her. Grass growing between the cracks in the concrete—"Look at that," Mother used to say of the tiny seeds flung from somewhere and growing in patches of earth wherever they landed. "Ruby, Ruby . . . that give us hope . . . hope!"

Pacing to the living-room window, Ruby saw her special tree, heavy with leaves that curtained the entrance of the brownstone across the street. It bobbed and bent under the heavy rain, its fragrance pleasing, yet achingly nostalgic. Everything happened so quickly. A short time ago, it had barely begun to bud.

Was it so short a time? I hadn't known Daphne then . . . not really known her . . . she was attractive, so attractive . . . tall, lean, lovely . . . such good taste . . . such lovely eyes . . . now . . . now . . . I feel for her so deeply . . . I can no longer see her.

Despite the rain, Calvin came home for dinner. He was out of temper. Miss Effie's presence was turning sour, but Calvin had decided that Sunday was his day with his children, and a little rain wouldn't stop him from keeping up the pretense.

"A bull," Phyllisia said when she heard the door slam. She had been hoping he would stay away. She wanted to stay in her room and give Miss Effie the cold-ass. Now she had to bathe, dress, and pretend to be civil. "From now on, I'm going to call Calvin Cathy Papa Bull-Ass."

It was a day when Ruby saw everything, everyone, with an unusual clarity. Phyllisia was the master of duplicity. It had to be impossible to hate Miss Effie as much as Phyllisia claimed to and yet eat so much of her cooking. Calvin was a vain man, using a woman he disliked to gain his ends. Daphne said he was not intelligent, that he was a peasant, a male chauvinist who shook his male organs around to gain what he couldn't gain with his brain. But he had apparently succeeded with Miss Effie without his male organ. And Miss Effie? Ruby looked at the straight-backed, pompous woman who didn't belong here. Miss Effie was lonely and in love.

But even being aware of this, Ruby couldn't stomach her cooking. The muskiness that Miss Effie had brought in with her this morning seemed to permeate the food. Eating would make her throw up.

"What's the matter with you?" Calvin, his chin greasy, sat, knife and fork poised, ready to dig in again. "You sick? How come you ain't eating. You like fish—and is good fish."

"It's the weather." Miss Effie answered for Ruby. "She has been acting so all day. It is so weather affect some people. Sometimes it's the bones, other times it's the spirit."

Calvin sucked his back teeth with little chupps, low enough not to reach Miss Effie. He was packing his mouth with food when the telephone rang. Going to the phone, he picked it up, waited until he had swallowed to answer. "It's for you," he told Ruby.

For a moment Ruby did not move. Then, slowly, she got up, counted her steps deliberately to prevent herself from running, counted her fingers before she raised the receiver, and spoke slowly.

"Ye—es?"

"Ruby, it's Consuela." Ruby gripped the phone, waiting a few seconds to let her disappointment drop from her throat back into her stomach.

"Consuela, how are you?"

"I won't keep you if you're eating. But my wedding day has been set. It's in June. I want you to be one of my bridesmaids."

"I'll ask my father." Her voice was noncommittal. How did she know if she was going to be alive in June? If she could walk down an aisle with a bunch of flowers? "Will you still be in school?"

"Only until the finals. My father doesn't think it's important to go back after."

"Oh—are you happy?"

"Happy? I suppose so. I guess the excitement comes later."

Thinking of Consuela's placid face, Ruby wondered how her friend would look if she were really happy, really excited, if the touch of long fingers could send her out of her mind with pleasure. She could not imagine Consuela like that. Perhaps that was the way the world should be. Placid, tranquil.

After Calvin had gone, Phyllisia, satiated by too much food, spread out on the couch and stared sluggishly at the television, her senses too dulled to tease Miss Effie. Hating her sister for such gluttony, Ruby went into the sewing room to see if she could arrange to sleep there, away from Phyllisia. Her sister's capitulation disgusted her. Like Consuela's planned marriage, it showed lack of will. They were both complaisant puppets, betrayers.

But am I different? I am letting Daddy manipulate me . . . do what he wants? What if I go? It doesn't really matter if she rejects me. I can call . . . at least I can call. I know love . . . I know love.

She went back to the dining room, picked up the receiver, dialed. She stood listening to the ringing.

"Who are you calling, dearie?"

Rage shook her. Her hand tightened on the receiver. Who was this woman who invaded her privacy so? She wanted to kill her.

"I ask who—"

"Someone she wants to talk to," snapped Phyllisia, coming out of her lethargy. So simple, but Ruby had not thought of the right words. Her anger receded. Replacing the receiver, she stood in the darkened dining room looking at the mural effect created by the bright light of the television. Miss Effie, broad, stoic, affirmatively sat before the set. Phyllisia sprawled ill-at-ease on the couch. The effect was comical. The puppets.

Ruby squinted. She tried to squeeze herself into the diminishing scene. It grew smaller, smaller, until she was absorbed, without substance.

The doorbell rang. She opened her eyes, forced herself to examine her body, feet, legs, hands. She touched her face. She was there, all there, alive. She looked at the scene before her. It was intact. No one had moved. The bell rang but no one had moved. She backed away to the door and opened it.

A stranger stood there. A beloved stranger, shrouded in a dripping raincoat and hat, staring at her. A stranger whose likeness to herself was uncanny. A brooding face, free of arrogance, pride nibbled away, marked by uncertainty, pain, contrition, yearning.

"I—I—it's a bitch of a day out there. It's just such a bitch of a day."

And they were in each other's arms, part Ruby and part Daphne, whole again, with substance again, people again, making sense again. Together, together again.

PART TWO

14

"It is said that man's greatest invention is the wheel. I accept that symbolically as well as actually. To my mind we are all cogs in one giant wheel, and it will take everything we've got to make that wheel turn smoothly. Man is stuck in a rut from which he must emerge to get on the highways of progress. If he fails, we are all, every one of us, doomed."

Daphne lay propped on the pillows at the head of the bed. She was playing with Ruby's hair. Phyllisia, elbows on thighs, chin in hand, kneeled at the foot of the bed, concentration tightening her face as she, weighed down by Miss Effie's heavy dinner, struggled to challenge Daphne.

Later she would be angry. Long after Daphne left and far into the week she would be thinking up arguments that might have told Daphne off. She did her best, considering her dullness. "Look, Daphne, there are two kinds of people in the world. There are blacks and there are whites. It is ridiculous to say that they are all part of the same wheel. Whites have oppressed blacks ever since . . ."

"Only blacks?"

"The Third World, Daphne—the Third World!"

"The Third World does not happen to be black any more than it is white. It is made up of peoples as proud of their identities as blacks claim to be of theirs."

"You know what I mean."

"I know what you are trying to say, but I don't accept your premise. Had you said the world is divided into the oppressors and the oppressed . . ."

"That is not the point," Phyllisia insisted. "You are trying to show me how man is all part of one wheel. That's silly. Man is made up of two distinct wheels, in constant war."

"Truly, Phyllisia, I am quite sure that I am every bit as nationalistic as you are. But I maintain that trying to separate the world into two colors certainly is not going to solve the world's problems. Of course nationalism is important in bringing oppressed peoples together to struggle against colonialism and imperialism."

"It is important to know our history," Phyllisia stated, matter-of-factly.

"Of course, but . . ."

"And if we know our history, we know that white men have always been—"

"I am afraid we are talking about two different things, Phyllisia."

"If we know history we can control our destinies."

"Let us stop this discussion," Daphne insisted. "The idea of knowing one's history and deciding how important it is that a caveman used stone, and what it has to do with feeding millions of people in India or Africa, is going to take volumes of work—and at any rate it can't be settled tonight."

"What is all that noise in there?" Miss Effie's aggrieved voice, the rattling of the doorknob, silenced them. Between television programs she sometimes missed Phyllisia and thought she was doing her duty by checking up. Sometimes Phyllisia did go back to sit with her to keep on needling her.

"What do you mean, noise? Can't we even talk in our own room?"

"And I still don't see why you have to lock the door," Miss Effie called back.

"To be private." Phyllisia grinned. "You know what that means? Private!"

"I don't know where you children pick up your behavior," Miss Effie complained. "From such a nice family, too." Her voice trailed off, prim, desolate. Tiny nicks had begun to show in her disposition. Calvin had not been to dinner for the second Sunday.

"Isn't her baby-sitting time up yet?" Daphne asked. "Why doesn't she go home?"

"She's a hanger-oner. She can't get the idea that Calvin is tired of her. She's just hoping . . ."

"He has no right to treat her that way." Ruby spoke up. "To use . . ."

"If she likes it, why do you care?" Phyllisia snapped. "Miss Effie has to be treated by a man, and it doesn't matter if the treatment is good or bad, so long as it's a man."

"You are not nice." Daphne grinned, liking her. "The more I see and hear this family the more I wonder how Bronzie got mixed up in it."

"Whether she likes it or not is not the point," Ruby said with feeling. "People are not things. Just because a person is around is not reason enough to use them."

"Can't use them if they are not around." Phyllisia sucked her teeth. "Ruby, you are so soft. It would serve you right if Daddy upped and married her."

"He wouldn't," Ruby protested, her face burning. "She is definitely not his type."

Surprised by her sudden irritation, Daphne asked with quickening interest, "What *is* his type?"

"He likes people with class—with style. Like my mother."

"He likes light-skinned women," Phyllisia said brazenly.

"That's not true!" Ruby defended. "Mother was beautiful."

"But she was also fair-skinned," Phyllisia insisted. Then, looking at Daphne, she said, "You are his type. As a matter of fact, the first time he saw you I thought he was bound to go for you."

"Yes," Daphne agreed, "he did. We went for each other." And, laughing at Ruby's pained expression, she added, "That was the shortest love affair on record."

"Anyhow"—Phyllisia changed the subject—"getting back to the wheel . . ."

"Let's not."

"What about Chairman Mao's theory that the revolutionary should be like a fish swimming in the mainstream?"

"I am not going to spend all evening arguing." Daphne brushed Phyllisia aside with a wave of her hand. "You always mix your arguments. I speak about concepts, high concepts, utopia . . ."

"Look, don't give me that." Phyllisia remained firmly on the edge of the bed. "You were the one who said that you were a revolutionary and a nationalist."

"Do you doubt that?"

"Yes, I doubt it."

"Then we have nothing to talk about."

"Because I have you."

Daphne looked at Phyllisia in exasperation. She had had no private time with Ruby, and the evening was nearly over. "Little sister, why don't you go and look after Miss Effie and leave the revolution to the pros?"

"Who is better than Chairman Mao and Fanon, I ask you?"

"You newcomers to the movement can be very tiring with your Fanons and your Maos."

"They talk about equality, power to the people. What do you talk about?"

"I never dispute them."

"Yes you do; you set yourself above the people."

"Pray tell, how did you reach that conclusion?"

"Just look at the college you chose."

"Brandeis?"

"Yes, I hear it's nothing but a bourgie college. What are you doing picking a school like that if you are supposed to be one with the masses?"

"We were talking about the wheel." Daphne smiled. "I was talking about an efficiently turning wheel. Romantic rhetoric is moving, but it's passé."

"That's right, change everything to suit yourself. Daphne, do you know that you are a phoney?"

Daphne's nostrils flared. Her eyes glittered angrily. "Look, little sister," Daphne said harshly, "every revolution has its own momentum. The time for people to have their heads kicked in on the streets has passed. Causes lost through misconceptions are still lost causes. Now you make sure you are prepared for the coming revolution in your way, and I'll try in mine."

"Make sure that you are prepared in your way." Phyllisia mocked, getting up. "I won't be preparing in a bourgie school, that's for sure." She pushed a fist in the air. "Power to the people!" As she left the room, she said, "I'm just going to keep Miss Effie on her toes."

"I like that kid," Daphne observed. "She uses her mind."

"You always argue, but you seem to be saying the same things."

"Fundamentally, no," said Daphne. "Your sister thinks on a different plane. She is of the younger generation, but she has to do her thing." Daphne's condescending manner made Ruby ache to ask how old she was, but looking into Daphne's sage eyes, she didn't. Instead, they snuggled close, happy to be alone. Daphne broke the long silence to say, "I haven't told you, Ruby, but I wanted to tell you, for a long time, that I—I have been wrong." She laughed. "It's hard to admit, but it's only fair to tell you that I have come to the conclusion that I have been wrong about you. I've changed. Haven't you noticed?"

Daphne had become more tender. She was more thoughtful, gentler. There was no longer any anger between them. If possible, Ruby thought that Daphne loved her more. But then she loved Daphne more—loved her completely. She could never love again so completely.

"I—I had never admitted in all my life that there was room for people like you. But then you showed up a whole class for what we really were —a bunch of cripples just like Miss Gottlieb. And I was so angry, Bronzie. How dared I be so angry?"

That was the first time that Daphne mentioned that day. But it was unnecessary. After that rainy weekend they had been so much in love, so close, that Ruby assumed Daphne had forgiven her. Consuela had been absent from school more and more, and Ruby was forced to help the teacher more and more, and there was none of the former animosity.

"On the subway that day, Ed Brooks came up to me and said: 'What do you think of that mother-fucking Uncle Tom friend of yours now?' And I told him, 'It's just about a bitch isn't it? Just about a bitch.' "

"Can you imagine, me talking to that turd—about you! That was incredible. I knew something had to be wrong. He was just as much a cripple as Miss Gottlieb! Then I began to realize we were all cripples—American cripples. We couldn't have gone to the aid of that teacher if we really wanted to."

"I began to see us all clearly. I saw how society was shaping us in its image. Right then I started rethinking. Voilà! The wheel."

"Daphne, I didn't go to Miss Gottlieb that day because I wanted to. I helped her because I could not help myself."

"Exactly. You did the civilized thing. I believe in progress. Yet I had to fight through to the realization that this society was making crap out of me. But being civilized is being human. Bronzie, you are the nearest person to great that I know."

"Oh no!" Ruby laughed. "I was a blank. I thought of myself as a blank piece of toilet paper that could be used and flushed away."

"Because you were being decent?"

"I *am* blank, Daphne. Nothing is written on me, until I feel for someone like I feel for you. When you leave I become blank again."

"I don't believe that. You would have gone to help that drunk in the park or Miss Gottlieb or anybody else if there had never been a Daphne Duprey. And so, although you sound so poetic and I like to hear it, you are a most beautiful person—not because of me but because of you."

"What about one's controlled instincts?"

"I haven't thought it all out yet, believe me. Nothing seems to have changed, in fact. Miss Gottlieb is still a cripple. She will remain one until she dies. She hates you and probably will until she dies. But she will remember you. She will not be able to help herself. All of us will be lost somewhere in her fogged-up mind. But on her death-bed she will, she must, remember you."

"Daphne—the way you make it sound! It is you who are being poetic. I want to be like you. I want to decide that I am going to do this or that for this or that reason and do it because I've decided—controlled instincts."

"Don't Ruby. Don't start me trying to justify myself. I am too young to know all the answers." Ruby started. In admitting to being young, Daphne sounded fatefully young.

"Some instincts go deeper than we care to admit. And some that we think are deep are not as deep as we think. Why, for example, did I walk the street in the pouring rain that day? Why did I wait outside for a big black Buick to pull away? What if I had caught a cold? Died of pneumonia? Bronzie, I could have left this world on a hummer."

A hummer. Daphne's pet anger. Ruby didn't understand it. Pain, sadness, anguish at the terrible suddenness of her father's death—but anger? And as though Daphne had read her unspoken words, she blurted: "The waste, Bronzie, the waste. My father was a great man. Important! Important as yesterday. Important as today. And he would have been important tomorrow. He didn't get shot through the head or stomped to death or starve in jail for his cause. No monuments will ever be erected on his behalf, no words written of his struggle—unless I write them. Bronzie, he slipped on a goddamn banana peel!"

"Oh Daphne, Daphne." Ruby threw her arms around Daphne's agitated body, still not understanding, only knowing that Daphne needed her, needed her in a way she could not yet define, only knowing that it had to do with the nuances of death and life, fate and faith. And being deeply committed, she had to pour her feelings into her friend, her love, her life.

They sprang apart as Phyllisia stumbled into the room, having pushed hard against the door she assumed was locked. "That old . . ." Phyllisia started but didn't end her sentence. "You'd never guess. She's going to spend the night!"

"The night!"

"Yes. She fell asleep in front of the television and now she's too tired to go home. What do you think we should do?"

"Practice poise." Daphne grinned at the flustered girl. "You must always remember to be cool, calm, collected."

"Yeah, yeah," Phyllisia said impatiently. "Poised, sophisticated, cultured, refined, intelligent. That was telling Papa Bull-Ass off. I was so impressed I keep trying to practice . . ."

"Such compliments, coming from you."

"But we have more effective methods with Miss Effie. Ruby, come and help me heave her out the door, huh?" Resolutely she headed for Miss Effie.

"What are you doing, Phyllisia?" Ruby stopped her in alarm.

"Going to bring her sheets to make up the couch, what else?"

She left and Daphne stirred. "Well, I suppose I should go. Phyllisia is being displaced again, poor girl." But she did not get up. Instead they lay stretched side by side, listening to the sounds of the settling apartment. Long after Daphne had gone, Ruby, searching for Phyllisia, found her curled around her book in the shape she had cleared for herself in the sewing room, sleeping.

15

Getting rid of Miss Effie continued to obsess Phyllisia. "She's like a chigger under my skin. I'll pull her out if it kills me." Above all, Phyllisia was a private person. She had tolerated the loss of her privacy on weekends with bad grace. When Miss Effie began coming during the week, however, Phyllisia rebelled.

"First she brings her aprons. Next a house dress. She brings her toothbrush and sticks it up next to Daddy's. Next thing you know she'll be moving in!"

"Obviously Daddy is paying her to be here. She can't be coming because she enjoys *your* company. Even if she loves Daddy, you are hard to take."

"Love," scoffed Phyllisia. "That woman doesn't know the meaning. She's too thick-skinned. She wants him, yes. But love?" After a moment she added, "But she wants him bad enough to hang on. She'll get him yet. You watch."

"That's dumb," Ruby countered. "The way he stays out of her path?"

That was true. The more Miss Effie came, the less they saw of their father—and the less time they had to themselves. She usually came just when Phyllisia was settling

down to an evening of reading. "Come, dearie, what shall
we have for dinner today?" Then Phyllisia would pull a
face, crossing her eyes at the woman defiantly.

"Phyllisia, that makes you look doltish. What if lightning strikes when you're doing that? You would remain so
for the rest of your days."

Fuming at night, Phyllisia proposed her own supersti-
tious fantasies. "What do you say we take some strands of
her hair, her sanitary napkin, and her drawers, and make
obeah—shrivel her ass down to nothing."

"Then you wouldn't be eating any more of that good
food," Ruby teased.

"There is more to life than food. I would be learning
about it if she wasn't around."

Ruby did not mind Miss Effie's weekday visits. She had
been coming home late, and on those days dinner would
already be prepared. But on weekends, the house was a
house of intrigue. Secrets, whispers, eye signals, tiptoing,
the silent opening and closing of doors, creaking floors as
Daphne came and went. Locked doors, silent laughter,
snickering, whispered discussions, planning, reading, and
lovemaking—a world of activities carried out behind the
back of the television addict. Yet not one pore of Miss
Effie's insensitive body, not one rising strand of hair, indi-
cated to her that all was not what she thought. And now,
on weekends, Calvin avoided his house like the plague.

Phyllisia had Ruby and Daphne doubled over in laughter as she parodied Calvin. Coming into the room and
standing at the door with an apologetic, humble air, she
cried: " 'Me children! Oh God, me poor children. I ain't
spend no time with all you. From today on, every Sunday
I eating with you, I filling the house with people for all
you, I giving you me best, me time, and I giving you the
famous Miss Effie.' Then he leave she and he gone."

Ruby was happy. She loved the life she had worked out
with Daphne—full of intrigue, small dangers. They were
together, Calvin was at ease, and that was all that mattered to her. But she couldn't say or do anything to stop
Phyllisia from scheming. On Sundays Phyllisia waited to
hear him pass their door to call him. "Daddy?" And when

he walked into their room, she would ask, "You coming home for dinner?"

"I ain't know."

"But Daddy, you said you were going to spend Sunday with us!"

Knowing that Phyllisia had never particularly wanted him around, Calvin would glare at her suspiciously. "Maybe—you know I busy—but maybe."

"Miss Effie is coming."

"And I ain't know that?"

"She's moving in with you—I mean with us, isn't she Daddy?"

"How you mean?"

"I mean you are planning for her to be our—I mean, she's moving in, isn't she?"

"What makes you think so?"

"All the things she's moving in."

"Things? What things?"

"Things like—well—her nightgowns."

Calvin's eyes went blank. He gazed silently at the two lying on the bed, then said with finality, "Nuh, she ain't moving in." Then in afterthought, "And what it got to do with you?"

"I—I was wondering when—if—well—you don't think . . ."

"What you want to say," Calvin demanded, getting angry.

"I mean, you don't want us to start calling her Moth . . . Oh Daddy!"

"Don't talk damn foolishness!" He slammed the door behind him.

"Phyllisia, why do you want to upset Daddy?" Ruby asked.

"If he thinks he can hang her on our necks and escape unhung he's sadly mistaken."

Ruby did not want to get rid of Miss Effie, and she refused to take part in the schemes. She neither liked nor disliked Miss Effie; she was a convenience. "If you dislike her so much, how can you stuff yourself with her food?"

"It's not *her* food! *My* father bought it," Phyllisia said in self-defense. "He's supposed to be taking care of me, not her. I guess you don't see how much food *she* put away. Her backside is not that broad just from sitting."

And because of Ruby's objections, Phyllisia did not confide in her. Rather, she made Daphne her ally. Usually they whispered and giggled together. Daphne would end up saying, "I don't think that one will work. You'll have to come one better."

On this particular Sunday Ruby heard Daphne's approval. "You probably have the nerve, but do you have the subtlety?"

"I might not have your intelligence, Miss Duprey," Phyllisia bantered, "but I'll match you any day with cunning." She looked at Ruby, anxious to tell her, but Ruby turned away not wanting to know. Phyllisia marched out of the room to keep Miss Effie company in front of the television set.

It was almost time for Daphne to leave when they heard Miss Effie walk down the hall to the closet, then back to the living room. A short time later she knocked at the door. Daphne slipped under the bed to hide, and Ruby opened the door. "Ruby, is my nightgown in there?"

"What would your nightgown be doing in my room?" Ruby asked, looking past her to Phyllisia, who was trying to keep a straight face.

"Phyllisia and I have been looking all over. This is the only place left it can be."

"Well, it isn't here." Ruby opened the door wide so Miss Effie could look into the room, but she stood so that she couldn't get in to search.

"I saw it in the hall closet last night," Phyllisia said affirmatively. "But I haven't seen it since Daddy left this morning."

"If it was there last night, it must be there now." Miss Effie and Phyllisia walked back to the closet together. "Every week I take my gown and hang it so . . ."

"Did you look in the bathroom hamper?" Phyllisia's innocence aroused Ruby's curiosity, and she followed them to the bathroom and stood while they emptied the hamper and refilled it with the dirty clothes. Miss Effie went back to the closet. "Every week I take off my night-gown and hang it so . . ."

"The only place I can think it might be," Phyllisia offered, "is in Daddy's room."

"Your father's room? What would it be doing there?"

"I didn't say it was," Phyllisia said slyly. "I said maybe."

Hesitantly, Miss Effie walked to Calvin's room. Phyllisia followed and boldly opened the door. She switched on the light. And there it was. The nightgown was laid neatly at the foot of the bed alongside Calvin's bathrobe. The spread had been removed and the sheets pulled back invitingly. "You see," Phyllisia cried triumphantly. "There it is. Who could have put it there? You, Ruby?"

Ruby leveled an accusing stare at Phyllisia, who, to keep from laughing, rushed and snatched up the night-gown. She pushed it into Miss Effie's hand. "Here, take it. I wonder how it got there?"

"No, no." Miss Effie laid the nightgown back at the foot of the bed, smoothed it out lovingly. "Leave it, leave it. I'll get it later." Then, preening like a peacock, she marched down to the living room, Phyllisia behind her. Ruby stood in the hallway, staring after them. It was amazing to watch that woman. She walked to the living room as though to an inner tune, her entire being transformed, glimmers of hope sparking from her like a halo.

"How did Phyllisia dream up something like that?" Ruby was incensed. "It's a cruel joke to play on that woman. She's in love with my father."

"Bronzie, don't be a prude." Daphne laughed—could not stop laughing. "Phyllisia has natural talents you should help develop in her. I'm dying to see if it really comes off."

Phyllisia tried to outsit Miss Effie in front of the television set, but that was impossible. Daphne could not wait around to see the result. Determinedly, Miss Effie glowed right back at the set until Phyllisia gave up. But neither she nor Ruby went right to sleep. They lay in the dark-ened room, listening to her listening to them. They heard her leave the living room, tiptoe down the hall, ease their door open to assure herself that no inquisitive ears or eyes could possibly follow her. Assured of this, she hummed a happy, toneless song while she tiptoed from the bathroom to Calvin's bedroom.

Ruby slept lightly, upset by the prank, but curious enough about her father's reaction to awaken the moment he turned his key in the lock. She was wide awake by the time he passed the door and entered the room next to theirs. The switching on of the light was loud. And she could imagine how he looked, gaping at the waiting hulk of woman in his bed.

"Eheh," he said. The surprised silence was like a drawn curtain. "Eheh," he repeated. "But what you doing in me bed!" Ruby strained to hear, but Miss Effie's response was muffled. Then, "What? You crazy? Look, I work hard. I on me feet all day. I come home to sleep. I need me bed." The woman murmured, low, insistently. Then Ruby heard Calvin's gruff voice. "I ain't know what you talking. If is that I want, I man enough to ask." Was she crying? It sounded like a wail.

But of course that was the way it had to end. Strange how well she knew her father, his hidden kindnesses, his terrible cruelty, his lack of graciousness, especially when trapped. "Oh Go—od," Calvin addressed the world. "I pay the woman to look after me children. She come, she cook. She eat, eat, eat. I pay she. Next thing I know, she sleep in me house. I ain't say nothing. She take over me house, come and go like she damn please. I still ain't say nothing. God, now she want to take over me bed!"

What mixture of excuses, apologies, explanation could she give after a tirade like that? Still the wail continued. Was she begging him? Did she dare? Then Calvin's voice again. "Nonono. You sleep there. I sleeping on the couch. But tomorrow, early, pack your things—all your things, you hear? I ain't want you to come back for nothing! You got a house—stay there. You got a bed—sleep there."

Angry footsteps pounded past their door, shaking the house with fury. Then the house grew silent. But their bed kept quivering, and Ruby realized it was from Phyllisia's near-hysterical laughter.

A few days later Calvin walked into the living room where they were busy reading. Ruby glanced up and knew from his casual air that he was annoyed. "Ruby," he said to her, but he had a difficult time keeping his eyes from Phyllisia. "What do you know about Miss Effie's nightgown?"

"What do you mean, Daddy?" Ruby countered. She really knew nothing, she told herself.

"It was on me bed last Sunday. You know how it get there?"

"No." But he was not really interested in her answer. His instinct had guided him to Phyllisia. Miss Effie had probably been telling him the entire story of the Case of the Missing Nightgown.

"You!" he snapped. Phyllisia's head jerked up in pretended surprise. She blinked. "Me?"

"Yes, you. I talking to you. What do you know about it?"

"About what, Daddy?" Her exaggerated innocence supported her guilt.

"You hear what I ask your sister."

"Ruby? What about Ruby?" Phyllisia gazed questioningly at Ruby, who sat gazing apprehensively at her.

"Don't play the arse," he said crossly. "What do you know about Miss Effie's nightgown?"

"Miss Effie's nightgown?"

"Is what I say."

"What about Miss Effie's nightgown, Daddy?" Phyllisia sat up, her eyes wide.

"Who put it on me bed? Don't tell me you ain't see it. It was you bring Miss Effie into me room."

Phyllisia's comic-book expression of amazement cracked through Ruby's concern. She bit hard on her lip to keep from laughing. But Calvin's temper seemed to be reaching its limit. Ruby saw his hands working into fists, then stretching nervously to keep from hitting out. "Didn't you put it there, Daddy?" Phyllisia's eyes fastened on Calvin's fists. He waited.

"Well." She sighed. "Miss Effie came to me—yes—that's the way it was. She had been looking at television, then she got up and came back to me and asked if I had seen her nightgown. I told her I had seen it in the closet, but she said it wasn't there so I helped her look. We didn't find it anywhere so we looked in your room." She looked past him to Ruby. "Isn't that how it was, Ruby?" Ruby nodded. "And there it was on your bed, wasn't it, Ruby?" Ruby nodded again.

"When I saw it I picked it right up, Daddy, and shoved it into her hand. I said, 'Here's your nightgown,' and she said, 'Leave it there,' and she put it back, right next to your bathrobe, Daddy, and she smoothed it out like this." Phyllisia demonstrated by smoothing her skirt lovingly. To distract Calvin before the bright-eyed Phyllisia cracked up into laughter, Ruby said, "From the way she acted, we thought you might be getting married."

"What?" He whirled around.

"She was acting strange, Daddy. Are you thinking of . . . ?"

"What are you talking?" He stared from one to the other. "I ain't know what all you think I am, but whatever it is, I'm not!" He stalked out of the room, leaving them wondering just what he meant. Had they convinced him of Phyllisia's innocence? Had they persuaded him that Miss Effie had played a dumb hand?

When Ruby asked Daphne what she thought, Daphne shrugged. "He'll believe just what his ego wants him to believe."

16

With Miss Effie out of their lives, a sense of bountiful freedom prevailed. They did the same things as before—went to school, cooked, ate, read. Ruby spent afternoons with Daphne, came home at hours acceptable to Calvin, and they went to bed at the same time as always. The change was in their thinking. It was they who had decided that Miss Effie must go, and Miss Effie had gone.

Calvin seemed suddenly satisfied that they could manage their own affairs. He mentioned Miss Effie only once, and then indirectly. He came in one evening as Ruby was preparing dinner, stood looking at her, silently deciding whether to speak, then blurted out: "This business of me getting married—it ain't easy you know. Your mother, well, she was a special kind of woman. Other women? Well, to tell the truth I ain't met one I'd let touch her little toe." Embarrassed that he might have said too much, revealed too much of his inner self to his daughter, Calvin hurried away.

Ruby smiled when he had gone. He had told her nothing new. She was aware of those secret things about him, the secret places where he lived. He never had to tell her.

That Saturday as Ruby and Phyllisia were on the way

home from shopping, Phyllisia saw someone she thought she knew. It was in the red-light district, a section of Harlem crowded with prostitutes and pimps. They usually rushed through this block, but Phyllisia, seeing this person, stopped and walked back to her. Ruby stood waiting, and when Phyllisia came back she told her excitedly, "Ruby, I'm sure that girl used to be in my class." Phyllisia decided to check, dashing back across the street, leaving Ruby uneasy but unwilling to go back through the teeming block.

Ruby tried to keep her eyes on Phyllisia, but she darted through the crowd, disappearing into the network of gaily dressed, cocky, swinging people crowding the avenue. Whatever had come over her? Ruby stood trying to decide if she ought to run after her sister when she heard a familiar voice. "Hello Ruby, what you doing around here?" She looked up into a broad smile.

"Orlando!" She was surprised at the pleasure that suddenly rose in her. He was so handsome—she had almost forgotten. And he looked older, much older. "It seems that every time I see you, you look taller and broader." She blushed at her boldness.

"And you get prettier and prettier. I don't see you around the block any more."

"Well, you know." She shrugged. "I'm busy with school. My father . . ."

He nodded. "I see him once in a while and I always think, 'God, if Ruby only give me the word, I'll go up and offer my hand—and risk another bloody nose.' " She laughed. "What are you doing around here?"

"I'm waiting for my sister."

"Then you're not going our way?"

"Our?" It was only then that Ruby noticed a pretty girl standing behind Orlando, obviously waiting. Her spine stiffened. "No, I'm not going your way."

"Well, be seeing you around." He waved to her and rejoined the girl.

Ruby's face burned with resentment as she watched them walking away. God, how she hated men. They were so faithless. Orlando had stood talking trash when that girl was waiting for him. Ruby began to walk in their direction, keeping her eye on them, but Phyllisia came up and caught her arm. "Ruby, I want to show you something."

"What is it? I don't want to be hanging around here all day." But she let Phyllisia pull her to the middle of the block where four women stood talking. "You see that girl there?" Phyllisia pointed to a plump woman with dimples and large frog-like eyes. "I know her."

At first the woman took no notice of them, but as the girls stared at her she began returning a look so hostile it made Ruby uneasy. "Let's get out of here," she suggested. "Come on." But Phyllisia was already approaching the woman. "Don't you remember me?"

The woman looked Phyllisia up and down, her frog eyes unfriendly. "I'm supposed to know you?"

"Yes, we know each other."

The woman shrugged. "I meet a lot of people, honey." She turned away.

"God, I must have changed," Phyllisia said, shaking her head as they walked home. "But how can I have changed that much in two years?"

Ruby shrugged and walked faster, hoping to glimpse Orlando and his girl. "I can't see any change," she said. "You look the same to me, but I guess you're growing up."

"She didn't recognize me. That girl used to be in my class in junior high school. Her name is Beulah. The kids used to call her Big Tits, and she used to beat the hell out of me every day until Edith stopped her."

"She looks too old to have been in your class."

"She isn't old. She was in my class. I used to be scared of her."

"What difference does it make?" Ruby was irritated by Phyllisia's slow pace. Orlando would be gone by the time they reached their block.

"I used to be afraid that I might one day meet her on the street and she would waste me. But she didn't even know me!"

"Why didn't you tell her who you are?"

"I guess I'm still a little touchy," Phyllisia admitted

ruefully. "But I can hardly wait to write and tell Edith I talked to our old enemy Beulah."

They turned into their street, and the block, as far as Ruby could see, was empty. At least there was no tall handsome man escorting any girl. "You're still scared and you drag me into the middle of that block to gape at some woman that could have wasted both of us?" She walked crossly down to their building and entered without another word.

Still annoyed, she was in the kitchen putting away the groceries when Phyllisia came in with a letter. "Talking about chance, here's a letter from Edith." She stood in the middle of the kitchen reading it. "Edith's been sent to a foster home in Peekskill. She says she had a nice foster mother." Ruby banged the refrigerator door shut and turned on Phyllisia. "Look, if you are not going to help put these things away, why don't you leave?"

Phyllisia looked at her strangely. "What's the matter with you? I'm sure my asking you to look at Beulah didn't get you that mad?"

Ruby kept putting food away and slamming cabinets, but feeling Phyllisia's insistent stare, she glared back. "I saw Orlando while I was waiting. He was with a girl."

"So?"

"So! He was supposed to like me so much, remember?"

"Ruby! That's almost two years ago. Don't tell me you expected him to be true all that time?"

"I didn't expect anything from him. But love is something that lasts forever."

"I didn't know he was supposed to be in love. And anyway, who were you supposed to be, Griselda?"

Ruby's lips tightened and she walked around her sister. Phyllisia was too young to understand. Phyllisia went on reading her letter. "Anyway, Edith says that her new mother has invited me to come up to Peekskill and spend a weekend."

"A weekend? A whole weekend? Do you think Daddy will let you?"

* * *

It was not easy for Calvin to refuse. The relaxation in the house, the easy camaraderie since Miss Effie had left, the feeling of renewed confidence in his daughters, made it difficult for him to refuse. Then, too, he had an interest in Edith—a seemingly detached but nonetheless vital interest. Phyllisia had kept it alive by her singular and constant devotion, forcing him to share, however slightly, his responsibility for Edith's fate.

He hesitated. "One whole weekend!" His eyes shifted around the room, searching for reasons for refusing. "A whole weekend? Peekskill is a long way."

"It's not two hours by train." Phyllisia had obtained a schedule before she approached him. Yet his suspicion forced him to examine and re-examine the schedule she handed to him. He pursed his lips, walked up and down, stared out the window long and hard before eventually qualifying his permission.

"Okay. If your sister go with you, you can go."

He was still looking out the window. Phyllisia started to protest. Ruby silenced her with a glance, and it was settled.

A weekend. An entire weekend with Daphne! It was Memorial Day weekend, which gave them three nights and three days. Calvin took them to Grand Central Station that Friday night and waved good-bye when the train pulled out. Ruby got off at 125th Street. Daphne was waiting. "Make sure you take that three-thirty train out of Peekskill on Monday, Phyllisia. We'll be waiting." Arm-in-arm, Ruby and Daphne walked from the station. It was going to be a beautiful, free weekend.

Mrs. Duprey was going to a dance that night, and would return Sunday. "We'll meet for brunch—you two, your Uncle Paul and I. You should like that, Daphne. You haven't seen your Uncle Paul for some time." Daphne licked her teeth to look noncommittal while Mrs. Duprey gave her a wicked smile.

They watched her dress for the dance. Ruby sat on Mrs. Duprey's queen-size bed while Daphne helped her mother zip up. Mrs. Duprey was lovely—cold, distant, but lovely. In her black, slinky evening dress, with a necklace of jade and rhinestones making her gray eyes look green, her recently coiffed hair looking less brassy, and the makeup toning her skin to smoothness, she looked much younger than Daphne. And Daphne, needlessly arranging the thin strap of her mother's dress, kissed her on the forehead, saying with the slightest hint of mockery, "Don't let any of those very young men steal you away from Uncle Paul, Mumsy. I don't want to lose you."

"Don't you worry about this lady." Mrs. Duprey had lost none of her sarcasm, despite the softness of her appearance. "Just you keep Daphne Duprey on the straight and ready, and the Lady will give you lessons on how to live as long as I did and still be able to brag about it."

When Mrs. Duprey had gone, Ruby observed, "She talks pretty rough to you, but she does trust you. She spends so many weekends away from home, isn't she afraid that . . . ?"

"Mumsy is the one who needs looking after." Daphne broke in abruptly. "She does everything. She drinks, she smokes, even pot. If she wasn't of the old booze school I don't doubt she'd be on stuff, but thankfully she is a lush. For my part, I don't drink, don't smoke, will not experiment with any drugs. What does she have to worry about?"

"Are you afraid to try?" Ruby teased her.

"Afraid? No. But my father always said that to master any art means that in time the art will master you. I agree."

"My father drinks, but he doesn't get drunk," Ruby defended. "He smokes but it doesn't hurt him. He just had his lungs X-rayed."

"Let's put it this way. I might get a charge out of doing any one of those things. But so what? I don't care to. My thing is my mind. I get a charge out of knowing more than the next person. That might be a weakness like all other weaknesses, but it's one I choose. I take care of my mind. And just like a slob brags about what he's drunk the night before, I brag about what I know. I take care of my body the same way.

"Maybe I'm afraid, but I dig my fears. I will not go to a colony of lepers or among consumptives, simply because I believe that my good living has kept me immune. I will not put my hand on a hot stove, even though I know that burns heal. And I'm sure that any of those things will have less effect on me than drinking, smoking, or shooting up. Bronzie, I'm one hundred per. Haven't I told you?"

They danced to the stereo that night. They drank malted milk, ate hamburgers, and talked in bed until they fell off to sleep. The red light burned all night.

Saturday they studied and read. It was an old and new experience at the same time, for although they had worked together before, they had never been able to work so relaxed. They read, talked, and explained things to each other without thinking of time or expecting a phone call that might be Calvin. They did not have to snatch a bit of love, then dash for a bus. By the day's end, Ruby felt she had been there always, and knew that love was meant to be lived like this. And there was still Sunday and most of Monday.

They awakened early on Sunday, postponed work until Monday, read the paper, and dressed to go to the park. It was a hot, clear day. The park was crowded with out-of-towners, as well as the multitudes who had remained in the city. They walked a long time, holding hands, searching for a spot where they could sit away from the crowd. They finally found one in a little clearing which strollers skirted. They stretched out on the grass and looked up at the cloudless sky. "Just think, Bronzie," Daphne said dreamily, "by this time next year I might not even be home."

"Not be home? Where do you think you will be?"

"On campus—where else?"

"Campus?"

"Yes. Of course I might come home for Memorial Day weekend—but then that's not sure."

"You're going to stay on campus?"

"Of course." Daphne raised herself on her elbow to look down at Ruby. "But you know I'm going away. I

didn't get my letter of acceptance yet, but I don't
doubt . . ."

"You're going to stay away?"

"Bronzie. Whatever in the world? What did you think?
What have we been talking about since . . ."

*But it had never seemed real to me. It doesn't make
sense . . . people don't leave people they love . . . she
can't go . . . she can't . . .*

The pain in her chest was so unbearable she couldn't
move.

Daphne kept talking. "Bronzie, how can you ever believe anything I tell you if you didn't believe that?" Her
gray eyes were staring at Ruby strangely, disbelieving,
probing. "Have you ever really heard anything I have
said?"

*Herself . . . herself . . . that was all she ever spoke
about . . . her mind . . . her body . . . her philosophies . . . what of me? What about me . . . four years
without Daphne . . . four whole years?*

"But you want to be a revolutionary. Everybody knows
that college is for wealthy people." Ruby was using Phyllisia's argument, being spiteful, trying to change Daphne's
mind. "How can you be a leader of the people and go to
that—middle-class place?"

"I intend to work from within the structure," Daphne
replied glibly, loftily, annoyed with Ruby for having
taken her lightly.

"It can't be done. By the time you have finished, you
will be one of them."

"Some people change, Bronzie; some people can't—
like me."

"Everybody changes," Ruby charged. "What makes
you different? People, money—everything influences
change."

"You have no faith, Bronzie, you have no faith. Well
fathers, who would have thought it!"

But Ruby did have faith, faith that they would be together, love each other, support each other, find a happy,
happy life. She looked at Daphne, stretched full length on
the grass, staring at the sky, and a great love overcame

her, a great anger, irrational. "Thought what?" She felt
hysteria stir, begin to rise.

"You don't know me. You don't know me at all."

"I know you," Ruby cried hotly, angrily. "I know you
well. You talk about being a revolutionary, a nationalist,
but what you want to be is the president of the United
States!"

Daphne laughed, could not stop laughing. Ruby
plunged on. "If you were sincere, you would want to be
with people, go to the same schools, go to the—"

"Same jails." Daphne finished for her. "My darling
Bronzie, you simply have not been listening to me. You
have been listening to too much black rhetoric, too much
of Phyllisia. You believe, like the unthinking majority,
that revolutionaries are formed in the jails. That is not
true, my love. Malcolm X was the exception. This society
doesn't play—it destroys. It is destroying black youth every day. The jails are just there to make sure the job is
well done. Those people who are wasted by the society,
who pour out of the country's jails, can only be *instru-
ments* of revolution, tools . . ." She smiled, showing her
white, polished teeth, and said teasingly, "Presidents can
be revolutionaries. But then, you know Bronzie, I haven't
decided that's what I want to be. I just don't intend to be a
victim."

"People don't have to be victims just because they
don't think like you, Daphne." Daphne's teasing had
taken the sting out of Ruby's anger. "My father doesn't
think like you, and he certainly is not a victim."

"Victim number one," Daphne said smugly. Ruby's anger flared again.

"What about your mother?"

"Whoa." Daphne laughed. "God, you are beautiful
when you get mad. Look, Bronzie, Mumsy is victim number one too, but we had better stop before we get petty
and tear the whole world apart."

"But why should you say Daddy's a victim. He owns his
own restaurant, his own car."

"And his own cliché ideas of making it in society, a

petit-bourgeois mentality. Look how he wants to push you through college."

"And you still think I'm too stupid to . . ."

"No, no, Bronzie. I think nothing of the sort. I just don't think that you need it. Some people, like me, go to college to become somebody. Some people don't need to. You are already what you will be, or almost, if only you will have the confidence to understand yourself. You love people, you have strength. You need so little to make you the perfect finished product."

Ruby's anger dwindled to an ash at the back of her parched tongue. What was all the talking about? Could it, would it prevent Daphne from leaving? *She will meet a girl . . . a lonely girl . . . as lonely as I . . . whom she will help, whom she will teach . . . who will be faithful to her. And I?*

"Bronzie love, we have the whole summer. Whatever happens you are my Bronzie, the most perfect girl I have ever met." But Daphne had not said she would stay. She had not promised fidelity. "But I must say that you amaze, Bronzie—the way you lit into me, you had me going. I kept asking myself, 'Is this my shy little Bronzie, crying and wetting up the welcome mat?' "

Ruby laughed and everything was wonderful again.

Uncle Paul turned out to be a tall white man, gracious in his behavior and obviously in love with Mrs. Duprey. He was also charming to Daphne, who underwent a subtle change in his presence. It was nothing that could be defined easily, but the moment the four of them walked into the expensive restaurant on the south side of the park, Daphne became more aggressively solicitous toward Ruby. She held her arm when they walked in, pulled her chair out for her, and, sitting opposite, held her hands. Mrs. Duprey pretended she did not see, and Uncle Paul accepted Daphne's behavior, with what, for want of a better term, Ruby considered good breeding.

"Will you let me order for you?" Daphne flirted outrageously with Ruby, and Uncle Paul smiled.

"Permit me, Daphne. Don't take away an old man's

pleasure. I enjoy introducing my friends to my favorite restaurant." He beckoned to a waiter, who hurried over, treating him with a restrained familiarity that spoke of years of service. "Anton, tell us, the *plat du jour?*"

The flippancy, the exaggerated sarcasm of Mrs. Duprey was gone. She matched, if not exceeded, her daughter in poise and sophistication. "Dear Paul, we have not heard one word from Brandeis. It has been such a strain."

"Probably an oversight, my dear. Shall I look into it?"

"It would be so kind."

Ruby gleaned little secrets. Uncle Paul in all probability was the tall man she had glimpsed on her first day at Daphne's; he was married, and he and Mrs. Duprey probably had a home away from home—a suspicion supported by Mrs. Duprey's complete change of clothes. Daphne did not like, but tolerated, her Uncle Paul. She learned all these things while being charmed by the atmosphere and delighted by the food.

It was early when the women left Uncle Paul and began to stroll home. It was a lovely evening. Warm, fragrant breezes stole up the city streets, bearing hints of jasmine, gardenia, and newly turned earth. Shop windows were still showing the pastels of spring.

Daphne walked between Ruby and her mother, holding their hands, and Mrs. Duprey, in high spirits, was delightfully flirtatious. It amused her that despite their age differences, she was able to get and hold the attention of handsome men. But then, she had been in show business, and one of her leading qualities was presence. "Look at that one," She sniffed over the strolling crop. "He's good-looking but vain. If he ever latched on to a woman she would have a hard boat to row. Squeeze a woman dry and leave her nothing to show but stretched skin." And, "Now look at those eyes—beautiful, so beautiful—he'd bore a soul to death in less than a month. The girl he has is only interested in looks and probably pays for them." Or, "Now if I wanted a dull life, that would be for me—plain, hard-working, TV type: baseball, television, football, basketball, the works. All I would have to do is cook, clean house, and drive myself crazy with drink."

Click, clicking, swinging, swaying with the bearing of a woman admired, demanding admiration for its own sake. Knowing men because she had loved them, still loved them, she was proud of her vast knowledge of them and used it. "It's a question of survival," she said. "Everything is survival. These men will kill you or make you kill yourself if you let them, so you got to know." Click-clicking, looking over this one and that, smiling, wise, unattainable but highly approachable. "Even women who go to church on Sundays are only working for survival. They pray hoping, others hope praying—but baby, it's all in the knowing."

It was great walking with them, listening to Mrs. Duprey, realizing that mother and daughter were very definite people who somehow complemented each other. They had walked about fifty blocks when they turned off Broadway to Amsterdam Avenue.

"Now that's what I call a handsome man. Dangerous type." Mrs. Duprey's heels caught the rhythm of the quieter side street. "He'll give any woman a hard time and make her like it. Expects love, but don't want to give it. Maybe had one great love in his life and wants to be true to it. So every living being has got to pay. Loves to screw and screws the town down, but won't give you nothing but the time of day."

Daphne's fingers tightened around Ruby's. Mrs. Duprey kept walking and talking. "I see him all the time. He looks through me as though I'm a two-bit whore. But that's because I won't have him. Too much trouble for me. I won't touch it."

Caught in a dreamlike trance, listening to Mrs. Duprey, Ruby followed Daphne's staring eyes to where the man of whom Mrs. Duprey was speaking stood, the hood of his black Buick raised, talking to a mechanic. It was Calvin! Mrs. Duprey, realizing that Daphne had stopped dead in her tracks, stopped too. Calvin kept explaining to the mechanic, even as he glanced up and gave Mrs. Duprey the once-over. Mrs. Duprey kept talking.

"Look at him—the world's gift to women. He owns a

restaurant near where I—" She stopped, looking from Daphne to Ruby.

Calvin had suddenly frozen to the spot. His head turned slowly back to them. He eyed them, his eyes fastened on Ruby as full recognition hit him. She saw him move toward her like a giant avalanche, hurtling through space. Unable to move, unable to think, she stood paralyzed. One blow threw her to the sidewalk, then he was over her hitting, hitting. Ruby held up her hand, tried to cover her face. Finally she felt herself being half dragged, half carried, and then shoved into the car. The hood slammed down and the car roared away. She glimpsed out the window Daphne being held forcibly by Mrs. Duprey.

17

He did not speak. Even when he pulled her out of the car and dragged her into the house, he did not speak. She sat on the couch, quivering, unable to think. He walked back and forth, back and forth, his thin lips ashen with fury, his eyes burning with anger. To hit her again. The thin line between sanity and insanity was near the breaking point. Knowing it, he did not want to strain it further. And so he paced the room, the hall, the house, so that his fury filled it, kept her in her corner numbed, unable to think, to speak, to move. His madness hovered over her, death itself threatened her, compressing her into the corner of the couch, trying to melt through it.

Minutes passed, more minutes, one half hour, perhaps an hour. The fury wore itself down slowly, slowly, and then it was past the danger point. In the suspended time as the anger lessened in the house so did her numbness. Her body began to pulse, her heartbeat quickened, her mind began to tick out little messages. He had struck her. He had beaten her in the street. How dared he put his hands on her, in the presence of her friends, in the presence of strangers, a street full of strangers? She would not stand for it. She could not. She was almost nineteen. A woman. A woman in love.

Then suddenly she knew what she wanted. She wanted him to strike her again. She wanted him to beat her, force her to her feet so that she could run, run, never stop running, never stop running until she reached Daphne.

He stood over her. She raised her head. Their eyes met, stared hard into each other's. His unspoken questions hung heavily down toward her, not wanting answers. He refused to deal with answers. He used his will. "Go to your room."

It was not fair for him to use his authority, his bigness, his great voice, his towering strength to protect himself from the truth. He needed answers. He had to have answers. Brute force was not the force to shield him from knowing. But he willed her to be innocent. Her answers might rob her of her innocence, and with this he refused to deal. "Get to your room!"

No . . . the issue is not obedience or disobedience . . . the issue is me! My love! the needs of my body . . . of my mind . . . my need to be . . . you must know that I am not a child . . . that I do not want innocence. I want to live . . . to live . . . to live!

"Get into that room!" The threat brooked no denial. Habit controlled the strings of conformity to the force of his authority. Getting up she walked with bowed head, passing beneath his diabolical stare, and silently went into her room.

Lying on the bed in the darkness, she sensed his pacing back and forth, back and forth, holding on to his blindness, preserving the fable of her innocence, his weaknesses, his ignorance.

The clock said midnight. It was late. What was Daphne doing? Surely not sleeping. Lying awake, staring at the red circle of light on her ceiling? Waiting? Waiting for her? Knowing that she would come—that she had to come.

Suddenly wide awake, she sat up and knew that she had dozed. She had been awakened by a light tap of the bell—Daphne's ting. Where was Daddy? The hands of the clock on the dresser pointed to three. She went to her door, opened it, listened to the silence. Out in the hall she saw a light under her father's door. She tiptoed to his room, opened the door. He lay across the bed fully clothed. She had imagined it. Daphne would not come if she saw the Buick parked outside.

Yet she walked to the front door, opened it, stood looking out. Disappointment, sharpened by a dying hope held her there. She could leave now—simply walk out, down the stairs. It was so simple. Daphne would be waiting, had to be waiting.

"Psst." Ruby looked up as a figure emerged from the shadows where the stairs curled on the upper landing. Daphne! Ruby's finger went automatically to her lips. Daphne ran down the stairs. Ruby closed the door softly.

"God Bronzie, I have been out of my mind," Daphne whispered. "I followed you in a taxi. I waited outside for him to go, and when he didn't, I came to listen at the door. I thought he was going to beat you."

"No, no," Ruby whispered. "He didn't. He didn't even talk to me. He didn't say anything—yet."

"Look, you must come home with me, Bronzie. When that man hit you, I was going to kill him. I swear I was going to kill him. You can't stay here, do you hear me?"

And then Ruby was in Daphne's arms, her strong, protective, tender arms. She had been praying for this. She needed this. If only she had had it earlier she would have forced his questions, given him her answers, settled once and for all just what he intended to do about her lost innocence. But now the issue was settled, there was nothing more to say to him. She had to leave. Daphne had said it, repeated it. "You have to leave. If that man puts his hands on you again, I shall kill him. I shall kill him."

Daphne's house was ablaze with lights—the first time Ruby had even seen it so bright. An agitated Mrs. Duprey, still fully dressed, stood at the elbow in the hall staring at them as they entered. "Where the devil have you been, Daphne! I've been out of my mind with worry."

"I went to Ruby's. You knew that, Mumsy."

"The least you could do was call. How did I know what that madman might do to you?"

"It's all right, Mumsy. Everything is all right. I am fine and Ruby is okay." They walked into Daphne's room, Mrs. Duprey following. "He didn't touch her again, thank God. I think I would have gone out of my mind."

"Like I went out of mine," Mrs. Duprey snapped. "I have never been so scared in my whole life. And there was nothing I could do. I couldn't go to the police. What did you think *you* could do against that monster? When you grabbed that taxi I was sure you had already flipped your lid."

"Everything is all right, Mumsy. I got Bronzie out of that house at least."

"What do you mean you got her out at least? What is this, some kind of espionage?"

"You didn't expect her to stay there after—"

"Where else would she stay?"

"She'll be staying with us here, until—"

"She'll do no such thing." Mrs. Duprey glared at her daughter. "Are you out of your mind?"

"What do you mean, Mumsy? I hope you don't expect her to live in that house with that man!"

"That's where she lives. And that man happens to be her father."

"But you know how unreasonable he is. You saw—"

"If Ruby feels like putting up with it that is her business. She's old enough to make her own decisions. What makes you the great know-it-all? What makes you the one who must think for us all? To decide for us all?" She turned to Ruby. "Honey, this has nothing to do with you. You're an all-right kid. I like you. But that man is your father. Whatever decision you make should be between the two of you. I can't interfere."

"What do you mean you can't?" Daphne towered over her mother, her eyes menacing. "This happens to be my home. I can—"

"Daphne!" Mrs. Duprey drew herself to her full five-feet-three, and suddenly Daphne did not seem so tall or

so menacing. "I have never tried to run your life. From
the time you were old enough to talk, you pushed your
old man around and you tried to dictate to me. I wasn't
too intelligent. I didn't dig causes. I was a former showgirl
who didn't make good. I belonged to another world but
you could tolerate me because I was Mumsy. I let you. I
even looked up to you because I figured that your kind of
people were the right kind of people. And so I never
questioned that red light that said 'Do not enter.' That
was your thing and I knew that I couldn't do anything
about it. But I dug you had yourself under control—full
control. But you are losing your cool, baby. You're forget-
ting something damn important.

"This is my house too. I pay the rent. I live *my* kind of
life the way *I* want to live it too. Now, as long as your
highfalutin' philosophies contributed to that, everything
was cool. But having an old-fashioned, half-crazy, West
Indian, brainwashed papa of brainwashed mamas kicking
my door down because *you* decide that he isn't the right
kind of father and his daughter must live here—don't!"

"And I don't have anything to say?" Daphne fumed,
but Mrs. Duprey's nonstop verbal attack had squeezed
some of the rage out of her anger. Gray eyes smoldered
into gray eyes, but the point had been made.

"I have never told you what to say. I have never been
able to. And I damn sure don't intend to start now."
Straight-backed, Mrs. Duprey swayed out of the room,
her heels clicking. They clicked down the hall around the
elbow into her bedroom.

18

The next few weeks found Daphne struggling to find answers. It was a struggle she was not used to. The answers she came up with did not suit her, her personality. "We have to wait for summer, Bronzie. I'll get a job. We'll get a place."

That did not sound right. Daphne's life was school. "But will you be happy?" Ruby asked. They were walking in the park on their way home from school. They would walk and talk for hours because Ruby no longer went to Daphne's. Mrs. Duprey's rejection had cut Ruby deeply. Daphne's room was remembered as invaded space, the red light a mockery. Mrs. Duprey knew, had always known, that their friendship was more than an ordinary close friendship, had probably judged her, condemned her, hated her for it. She was filled with a sense of shame. Even when the woman was not at home, it was emotionally impossible for Ruby to visit.

"Happy, happy, happy," Daphne snapped irritably. "What's that to worry about, Bronzie? Didn't anyone ever tell you that happiness is not a normal state?"

"But what will you do?"

"Something. Anything." Yet they both knew that

Daphne was not the type to do just anything. Ruby remembered Calvin telling her that he had not brought her to this country to be a file clerk. She tried to see Daphne walking around an office, filing—it didn't take.

"I'd work, Daphne. You wouldn't have to leave school. I'd take care of you." *But what could she do? What could either of them do?*

Angered when she had not been met at the station on her return from Peekskill, Phyllisia had listened intently to Ruby's account of Calvin's assault on her. Since then she seemed to have ignored the brooding silence around her and continued to bubble ecstatically about her visit to her friend.

"You should see Edith. She looks great, better than ever. The woman she lives with is like her own mother. I'm so happy for her." Over and over, she repeated praises of her friend, of her foster mother, of the countryside where she now lived. "When she leaves, she will be eighteen. Ruby, do you realize that that is only a little over one year away? She'll get a job in a factory where she will make a lot of money."

A factory? Was it possible? But how to go about it? Where to look? She had to find out. The moment school was out . . .

Almost a week had passed when Phyllisia finally said: "Your father's got something up his sleeve."

"How do you mean?" Ruby asked.

"I know that man. I can tell when he's plotting—especially against us."

"Why do you think?"

"Oh come on, Ruby. Don't think after catching us lying to him he's going to come and go without saying something. No, no, he's quiet for a reason."

"After that awful beating he gave me what could he say?" Ruby had thought her sister too wrapped up in her own feelings to care about what had happened. But despite her excitement over Edith, Phyllisia had been noting things that she had not seen. It made Ruby feel better.

Phyllisia walked around the house thinking for a time before settling down with her book. "I don't care what

he's cooking up in that evil head of his. I will not let Papa
Bull-Ass send me home to the Island. I'll leave this house
first!"

"What makes you think he'll do that?" It had not occurred to Ruby, but now that Phyllisia mentioned it, it
sounded possible. Calvin had such a strange way of thinking. The next day in school she said to Daphne, "I'm going
to get a job in a factory as soon as school is out."

"You must be mad," Daphne answered. "What could
you do in a factory? Look Bronzie, things will work out.
Mumsy is coming around." Some of Daphne's swagger
had returned. She had obviously been working overtime
on Mrs. Duprey. But it didn't matter what Mrs. Duprey
said. Ruby could never forget the hurt she had caused
her.

"Why don't we get a place now, Daphne? At least start
looking."

"A place, with what, Bronzie? We have no money—and
working in a factory—trust me, things will work themselves out."

"I have a feeling that we should start looking around
now. If we wait, something might happen. I don't know
what Daddy might do."

But then for a week Daphne was absent from school.
She did not call. Ruby called at her house but no one
answered. She refused to go to Daphne's, afraid that she
might see Mrs. Duprey. She could not stand to see Mrs.
Duprey. Ruby suffered. Had Daphne's mother, then, convinced Daphne that it would be better not to see her? But
that would not explain her absence from school. Something had happened. What? What? Then on Thursday
Daphne did call. "Hey, I called to remind you to concentrate. Concentrate and always remember to be cool,
calm, collected." Relieved, happy, Ruby laughed and
joined in. "Poised, sophisticated, cultured, refined, and
intelligent."

Obviously Daphne was her old self again. What had
happened? She did not say. Ruby did not ask. "I'll be over
Saturday, then we can celebrate."

"Celebrate? Celebrate what?" Ruby asked. But

Daphne hung up without answering. The only thing Ruby could do was wait for Saturday.

But Saturday Daphne did not come. Her usual time for coming was seven, eight, at night—the time that was Calvin's busiest. But seven, eight, nine o'clock came and went and she hadn't come and hadn't called.

At nine-thirty Ruby fingered the telephone dial. At ten o'clock she called. The ring-ring-ringing pierced her, her ears, her skin, her head. It was Mrs. Duprey of course. She had stopped Daphne from coming. She had probably taken her out to dinner with Uncle Paul, making sure that they would not see each other. Mrs. Duprey had become her enemy. In the bedroom, Ruby sat on the edge of the bed waiting for the ringing which would mean Daphne had gotten away. At eleven o'clock she got up, dressed, and went into the living room. Phyllisia, weary from reading, stretched when she saw her. "Where are you going?"

"Out."

"Out where?"

"Just out."

"I don't think you should. It's late. What if Daddy comes in?"

"I don't care."

Phyllisia studied her. "Why upset him when you don't have to?"

"Who said I didn't have to?"

"I do. Look Ruby, whatever is on the bull's mind is still only on his mind. Push him this way or that and we might push him into something we don't want."

"What makes you think we can do anything to change his mind anyhow?"

"If he had made up his bull-ass mind, he wouldn't give us time to pee or plan." Ruby thought a moment. Where would she find Daphne anyhow? She went back to bed, but couldn't sleep. Every time she dozed she dreamed she heard the ting of the bell. And each time she got up and went to the door, opened it, and looked into a silent, empty hallway. She did not drift off to sleep until Calvin came home, and then she slept deeply.

* * *

Late Sunday morning she awoke, and going into the
kitchen was confronted by a most incredible scene. Phyllisia was in the process of fixing breakfast for Calvin. She
had spread over the table, the tub, the stove, an array of
everything in the kitchen—including dried codfish, flour,
onions, baking powder, and other things obscured by the
general confusion about her. She was determinedly setting out to make acckra and bakes—one of the Island's
favorite breakfast dishes. Calvin sat in the middle of this
uproar at the kitchen table, looking at her, forced to sit
there by her insistence and his reluctance to curtail so
unique and extraordinary an effort on his behalf.

"I won't be long, Daddy, and it will be better than
anything your Miss Effie ever made for you. Just watch."

"I watching," he replied in good humor. There was no
denying Phyllisia's special charm when she put herself to
it, and her effervescence had put a dent in his defenses.
"But me place will be ready to close tonight before I get
through this damn confusion you making." His eyes shied
away from contact with Ruby's as he looked toward her.
"I ain't know what I do to deserve all a this. Is true I ain't
been feeling good these days, but now she getting me
ready to dead."

It was little enough, but just his saying that lightened
the heaviness that had been stifling the house for the last
few weeks. "I'll help?" Ruby asked, wondering if she
might not undo Phyllisia's efforts of charming Calvin into
good humor.

"No, no, let she," Calvin protested. "Is about time she
show more than she brass about this place." And Ruby left
them to their mess and went about setting the dining
room for breakfast. They were going to be close again.
There would be reason for laughter in the house again.
She was pleased, so very pleased with her sister.

Phyllisia looked lovely coming out of the kitchen to
announce that breakfast was ready. She was plastered
from head to foot with the dough from the bakes, her face
dusted with flour. She placed a pot of tea on the table
along with the platter of acckra, fried gray instead of

brown, and a platter of bakes, which were almost burned. She was irresistible as she sat opposite Calvin, her face beaming, waiting for his compliments.

He sipped the tea. "Humn, the tea good," he said. Then he tasted the acckra and bakes, ate a few of each, nodding every time he took one. Finally he pushed back his chair, smiled, and said, "At home we serve something that taste a little like that. Only we call it acckra and bakes. How you call that?"

Phyllisia refused to be daunted. "I call it *l'accra, et du pain frit, à la Phyllisia Cathy.*"

"Oho," Calvin said with a bombastic laugh. "That's a blasted good name. So long as you ain't confuse it with what we make at home."

The atmosphere in the house was immediately lighter. Phyllisia's fears about being sent away seemed groundless. Everything felt right again. Phyllisia went for a walk. She wanted Ruby to go with her, but Ruby, imprisoned by the telephone, refused, even though the tension in the house had been relieved and it did not seem such a bad place after all. The phone rang. It was Calvin, probably calling to check up, but he said with a touch of humor, "Tell that other one she food weigh me like lead. I ain't bound to eat for another week."

Her mood was even lighter as she hung up. She was glad she had waited at home to receive the call. Everything did seem to be moving well. She picked up a book to read, then changed her mind and reached for the newspaper, waiting, waiting for the telephone to ring. And when it didn't, she dialed, stood listening to the ringing at the other end. She hung up and went back to the newspaper.

As Ruby prepared dinner, she sat at the kitchen table remembering the last few times she and Daphne had been together. She recalled every expression in Daphne's eyes. No reason there for her not calling. If anything, their desperation had brought them closer, if that was possible. They had been close for so long. They touched more, caressed more, their eyes told of torrents of yearning, of need. Then why no call? Why—for two days—no call?

Then it happened. The little ting. Ruby bounded to the door. No one. She peered up the stairs, and comically peeking around the curve was Daphne's smiling face. "Is it all clear?"

"All's clear. I'm alone." Daphne entered the house and walked jauntily to the bedroom. She had a new denim suit with a box-pleated skirt and a sleeveless top, and it added a note of strangeness. What time had she to shop? Her face had a devilish look, and under her arm was a large bakery box which she carefully placed on the dresser.

"God, what a time. I thought I would never break away from the celebration to share it with you. Where is Phylli-sia?"

"I've been calling you."

"Mumsy kept me hanging around for days. How do you like the suit she bought me? Crazy, isn't it?"

"Yes, it's unusual." Denim pants were popular with the girls but she had never seen such a well-made denim suit. She admired it, then searched Daphne's face. "What were you celebrating?"

"Two of the greatest events in Mumsy's life. The first is inconsequential—my birthday—and you will never guess the second." Daphne's obvious pleasure should have been reassuring, but somehow it wasn't. Instinctively Ruby knew that Daphne's joy had nothing to do with her. Feeling excluded, she shook her head negatively to say she couldn't guess.

"Mumsy won the Sweepstakes."

Ruby stared at Daphne. What did it mean? She tried to react with pleasure, but her only response was a fearful thumping of her heart. Daphne was so caught up she had forgotten Ruby. "Can you ever believe it?" Daphne laughed joyously. "Mumsy refuses to let me live it down. For once I was wrong. That's really what we were cele-brating—my being wrong."

There was so much hilarity in her voice, such a sparkle in her eyes, Ruby wondered if Daphne had been drinking. Had Mumsy agreed to give her money for a place of her own? Did it mean that somehow they could be together? "Did you celebrate with champagne?"

"Champagne? Bronzie darling, you know that I don't drink. But isn't it a riot, Mumsy hitting the Sweepstakes?" She shook her head in disbelief. "You see, anything in life can happen!"

"Yes?"

Daphne didn't hear. Pulling at the string to untie the box, she asked impatiently, "But where is Phyllisia? It's just like her to be out on the day that I choose to be generous."

As though in response, the front door slammed and they heard Phyllisia's footsteps rushing toward the bedroom. She tried the door. It was locked. "Open up you two!"

"How did you know I was in here?" Daphne asked as Ruby opened the door.

"Why else would the door be locked?" Phyllisia also sparkled with excitement. "Oh God—what a day!" Seeing the cake overflowing with strawberries and whipped cream she cried, "What is this, a celebration? Just what I need."

"Why were you so long?" Ruby asked. "You've been gone almost all afternoon."

"Yes, I was waiting for Beulah. She just wasn't around. I waited so long that people took me for a streetwalker."

"You went *there?* All by yourself? Are you crazy?"

"I understand what you mean." Phyllisia grinned impishly. "Every man and boy and some girls too tried to make me, but like the Rock of Gibraltar, I refused to be moved."

"Where was this?" Daphne asked.

"Eighth Avenue and 126th Street."

"That's an experience." Daphne nodded approval.

"What do you mean? Anything could have happened to her out there!"

"Like what?" Phyllisia demanded. "People making passes?"

"They could have killed you."

"For what? I didn't have any money, and I hadn't done anything to bother them. Anyway, I waited and waited and Beulah finally showed. Then I went right up to her and asked her, 'Don't you remember me? I'm the girl you used to call monkey chaser and beat the hell out of. I'm Edith Jackson's friend.'" Phyllisia smiled, remembering. "And you'd never believe it, Ruby, she grabbed and hugged me! Can you imagine Beulah hugging me? Boy, it's a funny world."

"It certainly is," Daphne agreed. "The most impossible things can happen. Now why don't you get a knife for this cake—some plates and forks too."

"But what are we celebrating?"

"Two things, m'love: my mother hit the Sweepstakes, number one, and two—my birthday."

"How old are you?"

"How old do you want?" Daphne said glibly. Then noticing the inquiry deepening in Ruby's eyes she said quietly, "I am seventeen today."

"Seventeen! Is that all? You look way older."

"Child prodigy." Daphne pointed to herself.

"I'm almost as old as you." Phyllisia sneered disrespectfully. "I thought you were at least as old as Ruby."

"That has nothing to do with the time of day." Daphne tried to wipe the smirk off Phyllisia's face. "It's simply the difference between reading Doc Savage and Shakespeare."

"What about Dostoevsky? I'm deep into him now."

"Well, of course."

"Try him, you'll like him." Phyllisia ducked out the door.

"She has the makings of one determined to remain a brat the rest of her life."

A coldness gripped Ruby's chest, making it impossible to laugh. A strange opening at the pit of her stomach made her feel suddenly empty. She forced herself to smile, even though it was hard to breathe. "You're only seventeen?" She heard the incredulity in her voice although she tried to still it. But Daphne had been waiting for her reaction.

"No, I'm a hundred and seventeen." She spoke seriously. "But don't tell your sister—she'll never believe it." Then, grabbing Ruby in her arms, she buried her face in her neck. "And if that's important to you I'll be a hundred and nineteen or twenty—you name it."

With a movement of her eyelashes, Ruby batted away the strange thought that had begun to form in her mind. She felt the hot passionate breath on her neck, the strong arms around her, and every thought had to wait its time. This was not the time to think.

Yet as the three girls ate the cake, drank milk, Ruby found herself comparing Daphne with Phyllisia, tried to see the bond of their ages in their talk, their laughter. And as the two personalities asserted themselves in their normal behavioral patterns—Phyllisia with her childish prattle, Daphne with the sureness of her superior knowledge, the arrogant movements of her tall, well-developed body—her coldness disappeared and her smile deepened into warm, pure laughter.

"And what would you have done if that Beulah had snatched you when you told her the kids used to call her Big Tits?" Daphne asked. And Phyllisia, her long, lean, undeveloped body twined carelessly around the chair, her face smeared with whipped cream, answered airily, "Then I would have been one snatched chick."

"Instead she welcomed you. I wonder why?"

"Because they share a past," Ruby offered. "Phyllisia is nothing but a little girl to her now, and I suppose we all need a past."

"Can you imagine." Phyllisia laughed. "I have a past!" She put a piece of cake in her mouth and at that moment they heard the front door slam and footsteps, loud talking, and louder laughter filled the house.

The three girls stared at the door. What was Calvin doing home now? It was the busiest time at his place. Footsteps headed down the hall, stopped at their door. The knob turned. They stared. The door was locked. They breathed easier. "What the door doing locked?" Calvin called. "Open up—open up!"

Daphne slipped quietly under the bed, taking her cake

and milk with her. Ruby and Phyllisia crammed their remaining cake in their mouths. "Come on, come on—we got people in here."

Ruby swallowed from a mouth gone dry, the cake stuck in her throat. She drank some milk. It went down the wrong way, and she spluttered. Phyllisia slapped her back. "What all you doing?" He rattled the doorknob. "Open up!"

Ruby went to the door, but in looking around the room spied the cake box on the dresser. She grabbed it, pushed it under the bed. She hastily wiped Phyllisia's cream-smeared face. The cream stuck and she spit on the hanky and scrubbed. All the while the knob was rattling, the voice demanding, "What is this? You ain't hear me in there? You deaf?"

Ruby unlocked the door, but the front bell rang and Calvin went to answer it. More footsteps, loud greetings, Calvin's surprised exclamation: "But what is this? Is a fete for truth!"

Then he was back pushing the door, stumbling into the room from the weight of his push. He regained his balance, looked around suspiciously. "What the hell is going on in here?"

In the waiting silence Ruby heard Daphne swallow, heard her shift. She stared at her father. He returned the stare, grew more suspicious, searched this time, and discovered the plates with their crumbs and the milk glasses. "Oho, is that what you doing?" he demanded. "But ain't I tell you I don't want you to eat in your room? What you want, roaches to take we away?"

Then like an apparition out of their past, Miss Effie's broad face appeared over his shoulder. "Come dearie." She pulled back her lips in a proper smile. "Come help me in the kitchen. This is a surprise party I arranged for dear Calvin's birthday."

19

Miss Effie kept Ruby and Phyllisia rushing from kitchen to dining room with platters of hot food—meat patties, acckras, and hors d'oeuvres which appeared under deft, untiring hands. And Calvin's friends kept coming. No sooner did one group enter and settle than the bell rang again. Never before had there been such a mixture of Americans and Islanders in their house, and the girls were surprised he had so many friends. News of the party had spread by word of mouth, and the surprise which was to have taken Calvin away from his work for "a couple of hours" threatened to become an all-night binge, encouraged by the amount of food Miss Effie kept preparing and the number of bottles of rum and whisky that kept appearing. The effect was to make a nightmare of Daphne's celebrations, a jungle of the apartment, and a cage out of Ruby's room, a cage in which Daphne stalked angrily.

"If you or anyone else thinks I am going to be imprisoned in this room, you and they are absolutely mad," she said calmly as Ruby looked in on her.

"It isn't going to take long, Daphne," Ruby pleaded. "I

will be back after the food is on the table. It can't take much longer."

But people kept coming, food kept appearing, and the party grew more and more hearty, despite Calvin's protest. "I tell you that woman got nails in her head for brains. She spring a party on me like a trap. Who got time for party? I a working man. You know what I always say, 'Money don't make me, I make money.' But is in me place I make it and not in me home."

"Grandstanding," an Islander responded loudly, and everyone agreed. "To listen to Calvin he the only man who work. We all does work, Calvin. We all does work."

Phyllisia was angry and did not bother to hide it. She dragged herself from kitchen to dining room, a pout on her face. Ruby, worried that Phyllisia might act up to Miss Effie and get a backhand from Calvin in the crowded room, decided to take over for her. "Go stay with Daphne," she commanded. "I'll look after things."

Phyllisia disappeared. Ruby kept up the mad pace of getting glasses, plates, napkins, and food on the dining table and taking them back to be washed, glad that Mr. Charles and Cousin Frank had not come to ask about Phyllisia or to get her to sit and talk. As it was, only a few people noticed her. One man, talking with her father, called, "Hey, beautiful! Calvin, introduce me to that pretty girl! Is she your kid sister?"

"Naw," Calvin said, flattered. "That's me daughter and this me house. She ain't here to make friends with you, only to help serve you. Let she be." But he smiled at Ruby contentedly, deciding to forgive her, and his smile asked that she forgive him too. Ruby pretended not to notice. Why should she return his smile when the reason for her anger, his anger, was pacing like a lion in her room? One push of the door and she would spring at him, he at her, and they would never be able to forgive again.

"I refuse to understand it." Daphne was desperately holding on to her calm as she spoke to Phyllisia next time Ruby looked in on her. "How can that monster have his birthday on the same day as mine?"

"It's you who have your birthday on the same day as

he," Phyllisia corrected. She was lying across the bed, bored, and her boredom kept growing. Daphne, refusing to carry on a meaningless discussion, turned to Ruby. "Are you finished?"

"Not yet. I'll be . . ."

"Then I'm leaving."

"Please Daphne, just a little . . ."

"Ruby . . ." It was getting more difficult for Daphne to hold in her anger. "You are not a baby. And I am not going to stay here and see you insist on being treated like one."

"Ru—by . . ." Miss Effie's voice from the kitchen.

"Must you dash off every time you're called? Say you're busy!"

"It won't be much longer, I swear. Daddy has to go back to work."

"And I have to go and pick up Mumsy. I'm leaving." She went to the door.

"Daphne, Daddy is standing right outside in the hall."

"So what? He's just a man, Ruby. If he feels like taking me on, as he puts it, it's on him."

"Ru—by."

"Look Ruby, I'm getting out of here if I have to fly out."

"That might be the only way you will get out." Phyllisia smirked.

Ruby dashed out and down to the kitchen. "But where is your sister?" Miss Effie complained. "I bet she's in that room reading and letting you . . ."

"Never mind her," Ruby said, grabbing up two platters.

"I'm going to talk to your father."

Ruby rushed to the dining room and on her way back to the kitchen looked in again on the girls. "You had better come on, Phyllisia, Miss Effie is asking for you."

"Tell her to go scratch." Phyllisia did not look up from what she was doing, and Ruby noticed that the bed was stripped.

"What are you and Daphne up to?"

Daphne smiled. "I have decided to fly out." Ruby realized they were fashioning a makeshift rope out of the bedsheets.

"Are you mad?" They kept busy, refusing to look up. "Daphne, it's three flights down!"

"I know. I visit often enough to know. Bronzie darling, I think we need another sheet."

"Ru—bee . . ."

"You go, Phyllisia," Ruby commanded. "I'll stay here with Daphne."

"I'll go after I help Daphne get out."

"Ru—bee . . ."

Ruby stood looking at them helplessly, suddenly seeing their similarity as they worked, heads bent together. Young, silly, excited, adventurous. Eons and eons stretched between them and her, separating them into different time slots. Ruby felt she had never been young.

"Don't just stand there," Phyllisia said impatiently. "Go and bring another sheet."

"I will do no such thing."

"Then I'll just have to jump the rest of the way." Surely Daphne was joking.

"Ru—by. My God, where are those children?" Miss Effie's voice was approaching the room. "Cal—vin . . ."

"I'll go . . . but wait . . . wait . . . I'll be back." She rushed to intercept Miss Effie in the hall. "What do you want?"

"Where is your sister?"

"In the living room." She walked the woman back into the kitchen, raced with trays to the dining room, slammed them on the table, rushed back to the sewing room, bumped into Calvin en route. "What is this rushing, rushing, all about? Where the other one?"

"I'm just going to get her." She ducked into the sewing room when his back was turned, grabbed a sheet out of the linen closet, tore back into the bedroom, and knocked impatiently on the door. "Look Daphne," she said when Phyllisia let her in, "I beg you, don't do this to me."

"To you? What am I doing to you? I have to get out and your father is patrolling the hall. You can't have it both ways, Bronzie." Taking the sheet from her, Daphne tied it to the other two sheets, lowered them out the window. "That is long enough now. Look Ruby, either I go out there and confront your father or I leave this way. One way or the other I am going. I will not keep Mumsy waiting."

Ruby stared dumbly as Daphne and Phyllisia secured the sheet to the steampipe. Daphne had given her a choice. She could not stop her. "Daphne—please!"

The gray eyes coldly searched through her, through her fears, her insecurities, her love. She had seen that look before. She knew Daphne could be hard, cruel. What did that look see now? "Don't worry, my love, I'll be all right."

"I beg you!"

"We don't have all day," Phyllisia piped in.

"I said don't . . ."

"Don't switch from being a baby into being a grand-mother," Daphne teased. And indeed Ruby did feel old, estranged from them, their daring, their youth. She closed her eyes, listened to the laughter in the hall, the ringing bell, and suddenly all her old loneliness closed in on her. Why didn't she prevent it? She could. She ought to. "At least wrap it around the pipe again," she be-seeched calmly.

"Oh . . ."

"No, please. Wrap it around the pipe at least three times and then tie it."

"My square knots never give," Daphne bragged.

"Please Daphne. Please!"

"Okay, if it makes you feel better." Daphne got down from the window sill, untied the sheet, wrapped it one, two, three times, tied it, tried it. "Okay, done!"

"But it doesn't reach all the way now!" Phyllisia had been measuring the distance out of the window.

"I'll jump the rest of the way. Anything for Bronzie. One kiss for luck." She kissed Ruby's lips.

"Give me one for double luck." Phyllisia offered her cheek. Daphne kissed it and lowered herself out. Ruby closed her eyes and prayed. "She's down to the second floor!" Phyllisia called.

"Ruby!"

Ruby opened her eyes to see Phyllisia grabbing for the

sheet for dear life, her frail body slammed up against the
window casing. Ruby thrust Phyllisia aside and with a
quick movement caught the rapidly unwinding sheet,
twisting so that it wound around her body in one turn.
Then she stood, her back to the window, the dead weight
at the other end of the improvised rope dangling two
floors below, pulling her, keeping her in a death grip
against the window. Bracing her hands on the sides of the
frame, her eyes bulging with effort, her veins stretching
in her forehead, she stood as the sheet drew tighter,
tighter around her waist.

Suddenly, inexplicably, the pulling stopped, the strain
was gone. Daphne must have gained a footing. Ruby half-
sat on the sill. Her body began to pulse again just as the
doorknob rattled, and Calvin's voice, rum-tinged, called,
"Come out, come out! Your Cousin Frank and Mr. Charles
want to see you." Ruby could only sit and look dully at the
pale, frightened face of her sister, wondering what was
happening to Daphne.

*What did I do? Why did I let her . . . why . . . what
strange reason did I have for letting her take such a risk
. . . knowing I love her, would be lonely without her? I
saved her . . . I hope I saved her . . .*

"What the hell happening in there? Open up—open
up!"

She saw Phyllisia strip off her dress and slip, open the
door and stand in the nude except for her bra and panties.
At the same time she heard a man's voice from below,
challenging. "What the hell you doing at my window?"
And Daphne's reply. "One thing it's not, and that is to rob
you."

Calvin's outraged voice said at Phyllisia, "What you
doing, girl? You got shame, standing there half naked,
men all about?"

The voice below persisted. "I ask what you doing outside my window!"

And Daphne responded sarcastically, "If you will be
kind enough to let me in, I'll gladly tell you."

"I got my clothes dirty, Daddy," Phyllisia explained
patiently. "I'm in my room, changing."

"You damn better put something on your ass and come
back out of that blasted room."

Then it was all over. Ruby tried the sheet. It was slack.
She looked out the window. Daphne had gone.

20

Late the next afternoon, Phyllisia and Ruby went to Daphne's, Phyllisia bubbling with excitement over their daring feat. Daphne greeted Phyllisia with unusual warmth. "Welcome, fellow conspirer. Can you imagine? Here I am, still living and breathing."

"It was a close call," Phyllisia admitted, grinning. "For a moment I thought it was all over. If it hadn't been for Ruby's quick thinking—"

"Ruby?"

"Oh yes. I don't know what happened, except I couldn't hold on, and the next thing she was all wrapped up in one end of the sheet with you hanging on to the other."

"Oh? Well, Ruby has that gift of quick response." She looked at Ruby, looked into her eyes, said, "So, Bronzie, it was you who stopped the plunge. I thought it might have been my good friend Calvin."

"Calvin!" Then Phyllisia told Daphne how he had reacted to her nude diversion. "He was being sweet too," she commented. "There he was at the door ready to turn on the charm only to be set back to his primitive self when he found out his youngest was going in for strip-ping."

"I heard a man's voice from the lower floor," Ruby said. "Lucky he happened to look out."

"Oh him." Daphne laughed. "He kept staring at me asking himself, Is it a bird, is it a plane? No—it's Super-bird! Now I know what it feels like to be a sitting duck. Would be flying but lost my wings." Phyllisia joined Daphne in laughter. Ruby smiled.

Today they could joke. Huddled in Daphne's well-kept room, with its closed couch and open drapes through which the sunlight streamed, the terror of the day before was something to joke about. Yet to Ruby the terror re-mained in every bone of her body, every ache, from her temples to her toes. Over and over she experienced the agony of being held to the window, tied by the incredible weight that seemed destined to pull her down to her death, of her determination to be the link between life and death for Daphne. She felt again her squeezed waist, her pinched breath, her straining back, her moment of inhuman strength—all she had to give she had given. Yet how strangely her strength had fled. How weak she had become.

Sitting in the living room later, listening to the loud boisterous voices, seeing Mr. Charles and Cousin Frank trying to talk to her, she had been unable to hear, to speak, to serve. She remembered Cousin Frank's saying: "Is the noise. She ain't accustomed. Let she go rest, nuh, Calvin?" And in bed, unable to endure Phyllisia's excited chatter, she had escaped in sleep, a sleep that went on and on like that of the dead.

Now she listened to Daphne and Phyllisia go over and over the adventure, repeating details with slight varia-tions each time around. "You should have seen my fa-ther's face when I went in to my strip-tease act. His eyes bulged, the veins in his head stood out. I thought he would have a stroke. He didn't say much but what you want to bet that one day he'll catch me off guard and blast me one."

"Your *father's* face!" Daphne kept laughing. "The face

you should have seen was the classic clown downstairs. He thought he saw something fall by his window, and when he looked out, there he was face to face with a person. And get this. He said he has heart trouble. Fathers, can you imagine how lucky I was *he* didn't faint and fall out?"

They talked and laughed and Ruby listened. Listened to their laughter, their teasing, in smiling wonder, wonder at their exuberance, their youth, the strength of the new bonds that were tying them into friendship—a new great friendship that had only needed a shared experience, the courage to dare. At seven o'clock Daphne stretched, looked at Ruby. "Did you see your father today?"

"Briefly. He was under the weather from last night. He came home to rest for the first time in memory."

"But he wasn't angry or anything?"

"No, he seemed in good spirits—only a little tired."

"Well, that's the important thing." She stood up. "I guess I'd better get dressed. I have to pick up Mumsy."

"Do—you want me to wait for you?" Ruby's tone was uncertain. Daphne looked at her directly for the first time since they arrived.

"Oh no," she answered, and Ruby realized that she had expected it. "Mumsy and I are having dinner out. I don't know what time we'll be back." A chill numbed Ruby at her tone of voice, her smile. Daphne smiled more broadly. "That was as near leaving on a hummer as one can ever hope to get, eh Bronzie?"

The term was drawing rapidly to a close. There was a flutter and flurry about graduation, graduation proms, graduation clothes, among most of the students. For Consuela it meant preparations for her wedding. "You must tell me what color you want to wear, Ruby. My mother is going to order the material."

"It doesn't matter. Lavender, blue, whatever the others might not want." She had never really made up her mind about being a bridesmaid, but Consuela accepted it

as fact and Ruby did not protest. She was—had been—
Consuela's friend and Calvin would want her to accept.

But anxiety, deep, persistent, kept stirring within her.
Something had gone wrong, terribly wrong, with her relationship with Daphne. She knew it, felt it, but refused to
put it into words. They still rode uptown together. They
laughed, and talked and parted. They went separate ways
and Ruby kept insisting to herself that the excuse for
homework had passed. They needed new excuses. What
about simply wanting to be together? Daphne kept putting her off. "I'll call you later. I'm picking up Mumsy."
And she wouldn't call and Ruby would call her.

"I came home late. Went shopping for graduation
things. Did you do your shopping yet?" Ruby would
search her mind for trivia to capture Daphne's interest.

"No."

"When are you going to get to it?" Conversation too
polite. Strained. Wrong—all wrong.

"Can I see you today, Daphne?" Desperation forced
out the question.

"Mumsy is here. Do you want to come over?" No, she
didn't want to go if Mrs. Duprey was there. She did not
want the red light burning or the woman looking at its
glow with hostility.

"Why don't you come here, Daphne?"

"To your house? Ruby, you must be joking."

"Why? Why must I be joking?"

"Must I tell you?" *Yes, you must tell me . . . It was you
and me. We could have died together . . . It wasn't just
you. It was you and me . . .* But all she said was, "Then I
guess I'll see you at school?"

"Of course."

It made no sense. It made no sense. They had been so
close. Perhaps it was graduation and shopping and being
busy with her mother, who must have so much to do now
that she had won the Sweepstakes. But then say it,
Daphne. Talk about it. She had to find out.

Riding uptown on the train the next day, their bodies
strangely remote, no swaying together, no touching—it

was a painful avoidance. "Daphne, can I go home with you?"

"I'll only be stopping off for a few seconds."

"May I stop off with you?"

"Don't you have to report home?"

"It doesn't matter. I want to be with you."

"Well fathers!" Was that so surprising? "What in the world—can't you make up your mind whether you want to be a disobedient or an obedient daughter?"

"I don't understand."

"You don't. I'll explain another time. Bye now, Bronzie." A kiss on Ruby's forehead, and Daphne was fighting to get away through the crowd.

Nothing important had been said. Yet there was something final in Daphne's tone. Still, she had called her Bronzie. Didn't that mean . . . ?

Silence as nebulous as fear wafted through her as she opened the door and let herself into the empty apartment. She changed her clothes, began to prepare dinner, then sat staring at her upturned hands. Silence clogged her senses. She was only vaguely aware of Phyllisia's entering the kitchen. "I said hi, Ruby." Phyllisia shook her by the shoulder. "What's the matter, you sick or something?" Ruby shook her head, silently watched as her sister opened the refrigerator and began to make a sandwich, stealing sly glances at Ruby, who was too out of it to reprimand her for snacking. But Phyllisia's presence prodded her. She got up, began to cook—peeling and washing vegetables, seasoning the meat. She sat again and looked at her upturned hands.

Later Calvin came into the kitchen, looked at the pots boiling on the stove. "You sitting there, you ain't know this pot ready to burn?" He turned off the gas, stood looking down at her. "We ain't have time to talk," he said at last. "We must take time to talk."

The loveline crossing her palms was long. Long-lasting love, a happy love life. But Calvin was too shy to talk about love—her love. And Daphne refused to talk at all. "Frank and Charles coming soon—maybe in a day or two, and we will all sit down." He waited for her to answer.

Dumbly she looked at her hands. What did her lifeline say? Was that a short line? Or did she have the lines mixed up? "They tell me in school you doing fine—fine." He waited for her to finish the nonsensical examining of her hands, to look up in appreciation. Finally he left.

A strange man that Calvin. He wanted to talk—but he has never been able to. Not to her and Phyllisia. He had to have Charles and Frank with him to talk. He was not a child's man. He was a man's man, a working man, but not a child's man. He had been doing a job that somehow life had not equipped him for, and he had done it badly. Ruby thought of Mrs. Duprey saying that he screwed the town down, and Ruby knew it was true. Miss Effie wasn't his type, but he had types. He had needed Mr. Charles and Cousin Frank to help him through the years, to sustain him through their upbringing. He, Calvin Cathy, had raised children—had raised them successfully. A major achievement—a lie—a damn lie. Children grew up regardless.

And what would Frank and Charles have to say? What would they advise? Ruby, go to college? Be a doctor? Make Calvin proud? But she would never be an honor student again. She had proved she could pass, but only because of Daphne. What would they say if they knew she had had a love affair with another girl? She could almost hear Cousin Frank. "Well, Ruby, these things happen but you can put it behind you and go on." And Mr. Charles, easy, quiet, reassuring. "That is true. We all do things we are sorry for but we can't let that stop us."

Do penance for what? Go to college for what? To study? No! Her mind screamed. Not another year, not another month. Never again could she sit listening, listening to words, words, numbers, meanings, other people's meanings.

Daphne will not be here. I cannot face it . . . I shall not face it. I can't unless I'm together with myself, my most inner self. I cannot face life without Daphne.

Daphne was already in class when Ruby arrived the next morning. She did not look up from her writing when

Ruby came to stand over her. "Daphne?" Startled, Daphne raised her head, and for a moment they were looking through each other's eyes, looking deep into forbidden territory. But it was only for a moment, then Daphne shut her out.

"Yes?"

"You told me you would call last night."

"I did? If I did, I'm sorry. I was dreadfully busy." The heavily fringed gray eyes were smilingly indifferent, the face sculpted into a cultured mask.

"We have to talk, Daphne. We have to talk today."

"What about? Whatever for?"

"I have to know what is happening."

"Happening?"

"Between us. I have the right to know." She suffered openly. She exposed the dangerous, deep areas. Daphne looked around at the students beginning to stare. "Not now."

Calm, cool, collected, poised. Anger raged in Ruby, and panic. She wanted to jump at Daphne, scratch her face, cut through her cool. But she wanted, too, to fall on her knees and beg, beg. At that instant Miss Gottlieb dragged into the room. Ruby stared at Consuela's empty seat. She got up and went to the teacher.

"My," Miss Gottlieb sneered. "Do you want to brush my shoes too?" Ruby tensed, sensing she was a hairstring away from violence. Her eyes blazed but her voice was muted as she said, "I have no obligation to brush your shoes, Miss Gottlieb. I have only one obligation and that is to help you because you are a cripple and cannot help yourself. It is an obligation I have even for a dog." Miss Gottlieb looked into Ruby's eyes, sensed a force, a threat. Her face quivered. She didn't respond.

The day passed in a kaleidoscope of confusion. At one moment Ruby had distorted images of her classroom, but it was a room where she longed to hide away from light and life and people. The next moment anger, violent and unreasonable, surged through her, and she fought the urge to scour the school for Daphne, force her to listen. Somehow she felt that tomorrow would be too late. It had to be done with today. Yet habit forced her to drift from class to class, waiting for the day's end.

On her way to her last class she turned into a long corridor and saw Daphne and Miss O'Brien walking slowly in front of her. Both heads were bent, looking at the floor, hands folded against their chests as though guarding sacred papers, absorbed in deep conversation. A sudden rage swept her down the corridor toward them. They turned. "Daphne!" She shouted.

Both studied the set of her head, her shoulders, saw the flame in her brown eyes. A hint of apprehension held them still for a minute. Daphne recovered first. "Bronzie!"

Bronzie. Why had she called her that? She was a fraud. A hypocrite. Yet the sound of the name had an instant quieting effect. "I want to talk to you." She looked into the gray eyes, tried to read them, but was too agitated.

"Miss Cathy, is something the matter?" Green eyes, wide with concern, probed hers.

"I want to talk to Daphne."

"Later, Bronzie. I'll talk to you later."

"I want to talk now!"

Miss O'Brien looked from Ruby to Daphne and back. "Can it wait, Miss Cathy?" The pity in the teacher's voice drained away some of Ruby's anger.

"I'm afraid it will have to, Bronzie." Daphne stared at her, burning her into immobility, then she turned and walked away from her down the hall. Miss O'Brien stood uncertainly, studying her. Then, seeing Daphne disappear, she rushed after her. At the hurried movement, Ruby's anger surfaced again. She moved to run after them, stop them, tear at them. But at that moment, Ed Brooks came down the stairs and into the corridor. Seeing her, he blocked her way, leering.

"Feel like having a little piece under the staircase?"

She turned her fury toward him, saw him recoil and hurry off. Suddenly her knees buckled, and she decided she had to leave school. But it was only to wait outside.

Misery replaced her anger, and she paced up and down in front of the school. She had made a fool of herself. She had to apologize. Daphne had to forgive her, to understand.

I must know . . . I must know what I have done . . . what is wrong . . . I'll change . . . it doesn't matter how . . . if she wants me to be different I will . . . but how can I know . . . if she won't tell me?

Then Daphne was walking out of the door, cool, calm. Anger stirred again in Ruby, her body twitching nervously. How dared Daphne be so self-assured when she, Ruby, was in such misery? Oh, to scratch out those eyes, mar that face, destroy the fucking philosophies along with it.

Daphne came toward her, smiling. "Now, do you want to talk to me, Bronzie?"

They walked in the heaviness of the early summer's day, and Daphne was charming. She touched Ruby's arm gently to guide her across the streets, down the subway steps, gently, gently. "That's a new blouse," she noticed on the ride uptown. "It's lovely. It becomes you. You know brown on brown is my favorite combination."

Ruby's head swam with the compliment. What had she wanted to talk about? What was so important? She had been blowing everything up out of proportion, acted shamelessly. And Miss O'Brien, what would she think? Ruby's face burned, remembering. She looked up, saw Daphne's eyes, sharp, penetrating, reading Ruby's mind as it jumped from one thought to another. A roaring filled Ruby's head—it was the roaring of the train. "Can we talk at your house, Daphne?"

"No, but we can talk at yours."

Fears came rushing back. Why? Why there, after all that had happened? She looked desperately at Daphne. This was a confrontation. Daphne was forcing her to take a stand. She had no choice. Ruby pictured herself looking out her window at the lonely tree, the singular street, the disinterested passersby. She tasted the ashes of her love, thick on the back of her tongue. *How can I let her go? I shall never let her go.*

And Daphne, following Ruby's conflict with all its narrow twists and turns, allowed the door to open and close at her stop.

21

The big black Buick was not parked in front of the house. Despite Ruby's determination that it did not matter, she found that she breathed easier. True, he might come in while they were talking, but that would be different. She would have accustomed herself to the knowledge that he had to find them together. If he dared question her—question them about Daphne's presence in his house—she would let him know that she could not stay without Daphne.

Daphne, for her part, took no notice of parked cars. Walking with determined steps, she kept up a light banter from the subway to the house. "What do you think Miss Gottlieb does in the summer? I hear she lives by herself, has a maid come in for a few hours. Her family will have nothing to do with her. If she was related to anyone I knew, my suggestion to them would be to file her away in a nursing home in the middle of the Sahara, where shifting sands would wipe out any trace of her whereabouts." Daphne laughed, inviting Ruby to join her. "Don't you think that would be the greatest favor ever to be bestowed on the city of New York, on behalf of the teaching system of New York, on behalf of the student

body of New York—and it would all be done by nature."
Daphne went on. "Nobody that ugly should ever have
been born. Some people go out of the world on a hummer, but Miss Gottlieb came into it on one. She was an
unnecessary accident. An accident that the Board of Education saddled us with."

They entered the apartment and Ruby welcomed the
tension which silenced Daphne. She walked toward the
bedroom, expecting Daphne to follow, but Daphne went
into the living room, where she stood looking out the
window. Ruby gazed helplessly at her for a minute before
she said, "No, Daphne."

Daphne did not hear, or if she did, ignored her. Why
was Daphne exposing herself, being unnecessarily
thoughtless? "No, what?" Daphne said. "Just what are
you not giving up, Ruby?" Daphne turned to face her.

"I don't understand what you mean!"

"No, what, Bronzie?"

"Let's talk in my room."

Daphne laughed joyously. "Ah Bronzie, I look through
you to all your false determination, your confused loyal-
ties, and I really wonder if you think you are taking a
stand."

"Let's talk where we won't be disturbed."

"Is that what this is all about?" Daphne laughed again,
shrugged, followed Ruby to the bedroom. But when Ruby
locked the door Daphne objected. "Unlock that door. I
don't intend ever to be locked in this room again." Ruby
unlocked the door. Daphne walked over to the window
and stared out.

"I didn't tell you, did I? I have been accepted at Brandeis."

"Oh?"

Ruby tried to share Daphne's pleasure, but she was
secretly shattered, having hoped that Daphne would not
manage to make it somehow. "You have?" What did this
mean to them, what would it do to their feelings for one
another, now so tenuous?

"Yes, thanks to Uncle Paul and Miss O'Brien."

"Miss O'Brien?" Hatred for the green-eyed teacher

flared, glazed Ruby's eyes. But Daphne went on. "Yes, Miss O'Brien. You must have known that I was one of her favorite students. Brandeis is her alma mater—she graduated cum laude and all of that."

Was that really all that Daphne and Miss O'Brien had meant to each other, or was this just to explain the relationship for her benefit? "That's nice."

"Yes. Everything seems to be going the way I planned." Daphne kept on. "Just as I planned." She laughed. "Of course, Mumsy hitting the Sweepstakes was an added plus. But just think, I almost blew it all, just like that"— she snapped her fingers—"right out of this window."

It had been a mistake to bring her into this room—a terrible mistake. Daphne was still holding the window escapade against her. But why? Daphne turned abruptly from the window, threw herself across the bed, her hands under her head. "But that was only a reminder. You know, Bronzie, I'm so young and my mind has been made up for so long about so much, that as I go through life I'm going to need reminders." She looked directly at Ruby and said bluntly, "This is my last month in Harlem."

"No!" This was the declaration that all was over. No excuses, no buts, no ands. Daphne wasn't even going to be kind, to be gentle. "No—you can't mean that!"

"Yes. That's one thing about being dependent. Decisions are made sometimes that you have to go along with. And *that,* for better or worse, takes me out while I'm still ahead."

"You can't leave me!" But Daphne was determined to finish everything that she intended to say.

"Mumsy is giving up her job. She's buying a house in the Hamptons. She intends to live the life of a lady." At this, Daphne's full lips twisted in sarcasm. "With the help of Uncle Paul, of course, but then we can't win them all."

"But you and I were going to look for a place . . ."

"Mumsy insists on changing our life style . . ."

"We were going to be together . . ."

"She's even tied me into a sort of pact . . ."

"Daphne—you don't love me!" Tears came into Ruby's eyes. "Are you saying you don't love me?"

"She's decided to . . ."

"It's Miss O'Brien. It isn't your mother." Ruby's lips trembled. She was on the verge of hysteria.

"Mumsy has decided she doesn't want to put up with any more red lamps—in our new environment—at least for the present."

"It *is* Miss O'Brien, isn't it?"

"She's going to settle for one man, Uncle Paul—wife and all—but then we all must compromise."

"Daphne, talk to me, tell me . . ."

"I am talking to you, Bronzie. You just haven't heard. You have not been listening. You never listen. I don't think you can. You are too wrapped up in yourself."

"Tell me again. What did you say?" Ruby's voice took on a begging quality.

"I said I was going straight."

"But how can you? You are a natural—you told me . . ."

Daphne looked at her watch as though timing her statement. She gave an abrupt laugh. "For a time, anyway. Can you imagine my ego hanging next to the ego of a sonofabitch like Calvin? But we take a little, give a little —any mother-for-you can try."

Daphne's uncharacteristic vulgarity made everything sound final.

"No. No. You can't just turn off and on like that. You love me. I love you!"

"Bronzie, there is absolutely no sense in all of this. It is over. We are finished. I'm leaving." Daphne got up. Ruby rushed to get between her and the door.

"You can't leave me." Ruby tried to still the hysteria mounting in her voice; she struggled for coherence. *Cool, calm, collected . . . Daphne admired coolness.* "No, no." She swallowed the panic in her throat. "Stay, Daphne. Let's talk."

"There is nothing to talk about, Bronzie, it's over." And as Ruby kept barring her way, Daphne's face hardened. "I told you about my father, Bronzie. On a wide New York sidewalk, he stepped on a piece of paper. Not even a *New*

York Times, mind you. The *Daily News,* a fucking tab-loid."

"That has nothing to do with us."

"That has everything to do with us. Because you cannot stand up to your father, I almost left this world—on a hummer."

"I'm going to change, Daphne. I swear to God. I'm going to change. I'll leave with you—I don't care!"

"For God's sake, stop, Ruby."

"No, don't call me Ruby! Bronzie—Bronzie!" Her voice rose. Daphne's eyes melted into burning pools of sorrow.

"Yes, you will always be Bronzie to me. The most perfect bronze I have ever seen. There can only be one Bronzie. It took me a lot of thinking to decide that all I wanted to remember was your bronze beauty. You see"—Daphne spoke as to a child—"I am the way I am and you are the way you are. That day you helped Miss Gottlieb while an entire class waited to see her crawl at their feet, you towered over the rest of us—morally, spiritually—a real woman. It made me do a lot of thinking. Spiritually, the rest of the class was wrong, all of us, infected by this American society. You made us see that you were the best of us. Civilized. I have no doubt that you were right. I decided then I wanted to change—really wanted to change. But the day I almost tripped out on a hummer out that window, I realized I had been courting the most selfish, unseeing person that I have ever encountered."

"Selfish!"

"Yes, selfish." Daphne repeated and nodded to reaffirm her statement. "You want to be loved. You need to be loved. You *have* to be loved—by everybody. No one must escape your need for love, for pity. Right or wrong, your sister must love you, your father must love you, your teacher must love you, your lover must love you, and everyone else you catch in that net of yourself.

"From the very beginning I sensed that in you. What was the reason for giving, giving, giving? Yet such a de-manding sort of giving.

"Oh, you *are* good. Your reflexes are excellent. But even those are governed by your need for love. You would just die in a factory, Bronzie—you had better go into nursing, where you'll be appreciated.

"Thanks to you, I had to risk death to confirm the fact that I wanted to live—to be what I always wanted to be. I don't want to be perfect, to forgive asses like Miss Gottlieb for her ugliness. I want to hate people like her until I see them crawling—and I'll bust my brains out to get them there, where they deserve. That's the way I am, the way I want to be. Now, do you understand?"

But Ruby had understood nothing. "Give me time, Daphne," she pleaded. She grabbed Daphne's hands but Daphne broke free and swept out. Ruby ran after her, trying to bar her way. "Maybe you are right, Daphne. Maybe I am selfish. But give me time to work it out."

"We have had our time."

"No!" Ruby snatched Daphne's arm. "Don't leave, please. I can't live without you!"

"Don't be so dramatic, Bronzie." Daphne disengaged herself. "We have been good friends. We enjoyed each other, learned from each other. It is over. I want to live, and there is no life in clinging, pretending. We can't change each other, Bronzie. Our time together, all we had, is past."

She pushed Ruby into the apartment, quickly left and closed the door. Ruby heard her footsteps down the stairs. Ruby tore up the stairs, heading for the roof. She didn't care how she stopped Daphne. She would jump, land at her feet. Daphne hated blood. She would splash her with blood. Daphne would never stop remembering all that blood.

She opened the door to the roof, ran to the ledge, mounted it and stood at the edge, looked down, waited until she saw the tip of Daphne's shoes emerge from the doorway, and, insensible to everything but her great need, leaped.

She leaped, but nothing happened. And then she saw her father's ashen face, his blazing eyes, felt his firm hands on her. She saw his mouth moving before she heard him repeating, "You want to jump? Jump! Go ahead, jump! I'll put your tail back on that ledge and if you ain't jump I split your tail."

But he held her, held her tightly, squeezing her arm, hurting her, shouting. "Jump, jump, I beat you if you ain't jump!" And he pushed her away from him, got between her and the ledge, reached for his belt and started to unbuckle it. Seeing him in his merino and pants, his feet bare, going through the ordinary action of unbuckling his belt, brought her to her senses.

She recoiled, and as he pulled the belt from his waist, Ruby turned and ran into the building, down the stairs. She heard Calvin's feet slapping the steps after her.

She rushed into her room, threw herself across the bed, and lay there shivering. Her father came in shouting. "You want to kill yourself? I'll give you something to kill yourself about. Me. I the one who will give you—and that other one—talking—she think she got power—she bring she tail back in this house—I show she tail what power is all about."

Then suddenly sobs tore from his throat, big hoarse ugly sounds wrenched out from his insides, shaking his massive body. He leaned against the dresser for support, put his great hands over his face. "Oh God, oh God! I work me finger to the bone. I give she everything she need, she look good, she eat good, she live good, and yet she try to kill sheself. Oh God, why, why?" Tears seeped through his fingers and ran down to his elbows, big heavy tears that only a man could shed. "Why? Why? Why?"

Ruby sat up in bed. What had she done to humble this man? How dared she do anything to humble this great, big, proud, beautiful, awful man. "Daddy?" And then she was in his arms, caught in a terrible grip, a terribly frightened, crushing grip, a terribly frightening, crushing, loving grip. "Oh Daddy," she sobbed. "Oh Daddy, Daddy, Daddy!"

22

Who left this door open? Ruby, did you leave the door open? This is still New York, you know!" They had not heard Phyllisia's footsteps until she was almost to the room and when they raised their heads she had already appeared in the doorway. "What if your father . . ." Then her mouth gaped and bafflement changed to incredulity, a growing concern, a certainty that something had happened.

"What's the matter? Ruby? Are you all right? Daddy?"

Embarrassed at having been caught crying, Calvin turned his back to Phyllisia, fumbled in his pocket, took out a handkerchief and blew his nose. Hitching up his pants, he turned to Phyllisia, shouting:

"You—you. Always so busy. Always got that head in a book, writing, laying around the house. What's the matter with you? You ain't know you got a sister? That you got family?" Then, looking as if he might break down again, he rushed out, pushing past Phyllisia in the doorway.

"Now, what did I do?"

Ruby walked out of the room, leaving Phyllisia staring after her, questions, questions in her bewildered eyes. In the kitchen there was a dreamlike quality in doing the familiar, for the familiar seemed intensely new. Ruby was preparing dinner only to give her hands something to do. Phyllisia was in her room, puzzled and unsure about what was going on around her. Ruby heard Calvin in his room, moving around. He knew all. She held no secrets from him. He knew all and he had cried. He had held her in his arms and he had cried. The feel of his arms, rough around her, his hot tears wetting her cheeks—she had not had enough of his tears, enough of his embrace. His unspoken words had not been fully translated. With the moment gone they might never be so near to an understanding again.

Dressed, he stood in the kitchen doorway, questioning her with his see-through eyes searching through the eyes that were so much like his own. She nodded that all was well. "I gone," he said softly. She knew that all she had to do was shake her head 'no' and he would remain. She nodded again, smiling to reassure him.

He walked up the hall. She heard his footsteps come to their bedroom door. She heard him say, "Where you going with that book? Put it down! Lying around the house every day reading, reading. Ain't you know your sister try to kill sheself today?" And so having warned his younger daughter of possible danger, Calvin went out, slamming the door.

Phyllisia was a longer time coming to the kitchen than Ruby had expected, and when she did come she stood for a long time before she could bring herself to speak. "Ruby?" Her eyes ere round with disbelief. "Ruby, do you really want to die?"

As the dreamlike haze through which she had been moving suddenly dissolved, Ruby said, "No!" The question was so simply put there could only be one answer. "No, Phyllisia, I want to live!"

"Then why?"

"I—I was unhappy."

"Unhappy? Over something *I* did?"

"You?" Ruby looked at Phyllisia, surprised.

"If it was, Ruby—if it was something I said, I would cut

off my tongue. If it was something I did—I would cut off my hands."

"No, it was nothing you did, Phyllisia. It was Daphne."

"Daphne?"

"Yes." She wanted to talk to Phyllisia, tell her all. But no —that would come later. "She—we are not going to be friends . . ."

"Oh . . ." Disappointment tinged Phyllisia's voice. Then, realizing that Ruby would say no more, she shrugged. "Why let that worry you? She was nothing but a phoney."

"Phoney? Daphne?"

"Sure. Talking about being such a big-time revolutionary and then trying to get into that bourgie school."

"She was accepted."

"She was? God help us all—especially those kids at Brandeis." At that moment the bell tinged. Phyllisia and Ruby stared at each other. Daphne? Ruby, drained by weeks of torment, worn to exhaustion by the ruptured dam of emotions, waited for the feeling, the heartbeat of anticipation. Nothing. Her world had fallen into so many pieces. Tomorrow, the day after, she might rearrange them into a whole again, place the pieces into some meaningful perspective. But today?

"What do you want me to tell her?" Phyllisia whispered.

"Tell her I will call her tomorrow."

Ruby sat down weakly, looked at the pots on the stove. There was security in her exhaustion. It forced her to rest, to shut her mind to things better left to deal with another time.

"Ruby." Phyllisia back at the door, still whispering. "It's Orlando. He says Daddy told him to come." Ruby stared at Phyllisia. Orlando? What did he want? If only he had come before—months before. If only he had had the courage. *No . . . no . . . she was the one . . . the one I needed . . . she was so important to me . . . my life . . . Daphne . . . Daphne . . . yet she said I was selfish . . . selfish . . . selfish.* Ruby saw Daphne again, walking from school, her head high over the crowd, moving as though pushed by a strong wind, her long legs widening the distance between them, disappearing as she turned the corner, going out of her life.

"What should I tell him?" Phyllisia was whispering.

"I'm tired," Ruby whispered. "Tell him I can't see him . . ." Her voice trailed off, and Phyllisia hesitated at the doorway.

Ruby looked down at her hands, thinking of Orlando, the last time she had seen him. She remembered the admiration that had still nestled in his eyes. She put her hand up to touch her disheveled hair.

"Tell him another time."

And as Phyllisia turned to go, Ruby said, "Maybe tomorrow . . ."